THE HEIR OF VASILICA

A catalogue record for this book is available from the National Library of New Zealand.

Trade paperback ISBN 978 1 99 116586 2
Hardback ISBN 978 1 99 116588 6

Cover design by Grady Earls
Illustrations, map, and formatting
by Etheric Tales & Edits
etherictalesnedits.com

Design & layout www.yourbooks.co.nz

THE WYTCHLING CHRONICLES

THE HEIR OF VASILICA

NOVELIA

C.C. DAVIE

BEGUE
ESTATE

CORVIN

DAMARIS
COTTAGE

ALBA

EZRAH'S
COTTAGE

MURET

VECHNEA

MIRCIA

Pronunciation Guide

Characters:

Lyrik Vasilica: *Li-ric Va-sill-i-ka*
Damaris: *Da-ma-ris*
Vladimyre: *Vlad-i-meer*
Darius: *Da-ree-oos*
Kalius: *Ka-lie-oos*
Andrei: *Un-drey*
Gheata: *Gee-ta*
Toma: *Toe-ma*
Mihail: *Me-hail*
Kalib: *Ka-lib*
Emil: *Eh-meel*
Sorin: *So-rin*
Klause: *Klow-s*
Gwydeon: *Gwy-dee-un*
Astryd: *Ass-trid*
Rogue: *Row-g*
Faisyn: *Fai-sin*

Places:

Corvin: *Core-Vin*
Becue: *Ber-cue*
Vechnea: *Veh-knee-ah*
Muret: *Muh-rett*
Mircia: *Mer-see-ah*
Attica: *At-i-ka*

Other:

Prima Sotie: *Pre-ma So-tee*
Domne: *Dom-nei*
Sylvyn: *Sill-vin*
Drayvn: *Dray-vin*

This book is dedicated to my readers.
Sorry (only a little bit) for the cliffhanger in Wings.
As a peace offering, here is some more trauma.
I appreciate you all.

Content Warning

The Heir of Vasilica is an adult fantasy book that contains some strong language and content some readers may find distressing, including;

Murder

Misogyny

Mental Abuse

Physical assault

Torture

More Murder

A bit more murder for good measure.

If you need more detail on these, a more comprehensive list can be found on my website: C.C Davie Author.

CHAPTER ONE

Birth

It was the longest winter Mircia had seen when my mother laboured for four days to bring me into this world. I often wonder what she was like, but my existence is proof enough of the strength she possessed.

The seventeenth wife of my sire›s harem, a never-ending procession of gifted Sylvyn women that existed only to provide my sire with the coveted male child. Thrown away as easily as they were acquired.

I was the only child of the union between them, though my sisters number into the hundreds.

I had seven older brothers, and the day I ran from Mircia, every one of them was dead.

My mother was an Elementyl, sold to the Drayvn by her family to cover a debt.

My sire is Lord Vladimyre Vasilica, the uncontested, vicious ruler of Mircia.

I am the only female Drayvn to have ever been born.

Drayvn are feared amongst the Sylvyn. Drayvn feel no fear.

They feel no happiness. They *feel* nothing, except rage and a thirst for dominance and blood. Males rarely make it through gestation, killing their mothers before the ill-fated woman has a chance to bring them into the world. If the mother survives the pregnancy, it is even less common for her to make it through birth.

Females carry the Drayvn gene. It can sometimes make a male child more likely if the mother is birthed of the line. But a female is always just Sylvyn, sometimes gifted, but mostly just cursed to live the long, long life of a Sylvyn trapped in a masochistic society as Drayvn broodmares.

My sire had no use for female children. Three hundred and twenty-two years of life and countless wives had produced far more daughters than my sire could ever have use for. My sisters would have just been vassals, used for their bloodlines and nothing more. He did them a mercy, throwing them, just hours old into the snow for the wolves.

The souls of my stepmothers that had not survived my sire lingered there in the woods, waiting for those unwanted daughters.

I sometimes wonder if I should have joined them.

My sire was summoned to my mother's chambers after my birth, to look over his newest offspring.

"What is it?" he asked, not bothering to look at my mother's battered and cooling body still lying on her birthing bed.

"A female," the maester of medicine replied. He was a hunched old man, his fingers gnarled and bony where they held me, wrapped in a blood-smeared blanket.

"Throw it to the wolves with its mother's body," Lord Vladimyre said, his lip curling in disgust as he turned to leave. "And find me a replacement for it's mother."

"My lord," the maester was hesitant, ducking his head as Lord Vladimyre turned his cold, black eyes onto him.

"She is female, yes. But look." The maester had unwrapped my small body, offering me over to my sire.

He stared down at me, a long, claw-tipped finger reaching to turn my face toward him. I stared back with onyx black eyes, the image of his. The tip of his claw pierced the soft skin of my cheek. I had hissed at the pain, snarling like no normal Sylvyn child did at the hand that drew away from me, my blood glinting on his fingertip. His fangs glinted as his lips parted, his tongue licking away the red smear.

"A Drayvn female," he mused, eyes narrowing as he raked them over my small frame, then behind us to my mother. "There is no saving her? If she produces a female such as this, a male would be magnificent."

The maester shook his head. "She is well passed, My Lord."

My sire had just turned his attention back to me, not a second thought for the woman that had been his wife.

"Find a woman to raise her. I have no use for her until she matures. And send for her mother's family. I want any woman of that line to be added to my harem."

"My Lord," the maester cringed as he once again forstalled my sire's departure. "It is the Lord's right to name his Drayvn offspring.

Lord Vladimyre snarled softly. "Give her the woman's name, she no longer has use for it."

"As you wish, My Lord." The maester simpered, bowing over me.

I have no memories of this time. Just pieces of a story I have sewn together over the years from my parents, the women of the harem and Darius.

Mama used to tell me often how she was taken from the kitchens, her heart still heavy from the loss of her own child, Amna. The babe had only lived a few weeks, born weak with a heart that gave out in her sleep.

I had been placed in her arms, a purse of silver dumped on my swaddling, and she was ordered to return to her home with me. Terrified and only too happy to get away from the castle, Mama had fled with me, back to the cottage in the woods where she and Papa had taken me on as their own.

CHAPTER TWO

Age five

"Lyrik," Mama called from the window. "Come in for supper, love."

I was five. Papa had been away for a month working, and food was beginning to get low. Papa had killed one of the lambs before he left, and I could smell the last of it bubbling over the fireplace for supper. My stomach grumbled at the thought of the hot stew that Mama always found a way to make tasty, even when the cupboards were bare.

Sometimes a man would come to the cottage. Mama always looked scared when he did. It was never the same one, but they would always ask to see me, grasping my face in their cold hands and turning me one way and the other, as if I was one of Papa's piglets and they were wanting to buy me for their oven. But if I was a good girl, opening my mouth to show them my teeth, showing them my hands when Mama asked, they would leave Mama a bag of silver, and the next day we would go to the market.

I knew we were due another visit. Mama had that look in her eyes, and whenever I turned around, I caught her staring at me.

I was excited. The man coming meant we could go to the market soon, and Mama had promised I could pick out a new dress. Mine was getting tight and had sap stains on it from climbing trees.

"Did you wash your hands?" Mama asked as I fetched my wooden spoon from its hook and climbed into my seat next to the fireplace.

"Yes, Mama," I grumbled, biting on the rough edge of my spoon hungrily, mouth watering as I watched her ladle a steaming scoop into my bowl.

"Good girl," she murmured as she put my bowl down, stroking a hand down my hair, and pulling it out of my face. "Here, let me tie this back, otherwise it will go all through your food."

I screwed my face up as she twisted my long golden hair up into a knot behind my head, clucking softly at the snarls in it.

"Lyrik Vasilica, what have you been doing?" she scolded.

I grumbled as it tugged painfully against my scalp, yanking my head out of her grasp.

"None of that, or you will go to bed with no supper," Mama said sharply, her hands firm as she whipped out a strip of fabric with which to bind it.

I sighed, waiting for her to finish before tucking into my food, happily chewing on the fat-rich meat as she sat across from me, a small cup of it in her own hand that she had poured from the last of the pot.

"You want some of mine, Mama?" I asked around a mouthful of meat, huffing air into my mouth as it burnt my tongue.

"No, love, this will do me fine," she said, her eyes crinkling as she smiled at me. "Thank you though, sweet girl."

I hummed happily as I finished the rest, wiping the juices up with my fingers and sucking it off, earning myself another scolding from Mama and a wet washcloth.

She was nervous tonight, her eyes kept going to the door and she jumped at every sound, so I wasn't surprised when the heavy footsteps thunked up our ramshackle porch, and a fist pounded on the door.

"Mrs. Damaris."

Mama paled slightly, wiping her hands on her apron as she glanced at me. She licked her finger, wiping something off my cheek and lifted my chin to look at her.

"Just do what he asks, and he will leave again," she whispered to me. "Remember what I told you, no getting mad, ok?"

I nodded, giving her my brightest smile, imagining the lovely light blue dress I had seen hanging in a stall the month before.

I watched as she opened the door, stepping back to allow a cloaked man to step through the threshold. He wasn't huge. Papa was taller than him, but Mama shrunk back as he turned to look at her.

"This her?" he asked, in a voice that made the hair prickle on my arms.

Mama nodded, skirting the room to come to my side, a warm hand resting on my shoulder, squeezing reassuringly.

"This is my Lyrik," she said in a small voice.

The man huffed a mirthless laugh, stepping across the room. The closer he got to me, the more my stomach twisted. He wasn't like the other men that had come, his black eyes glittered as they fixed on me the same way wolves watched their prey. He reached out and ran a claw tipped finger down my cheek.

"Hello, daughter," he said in that haunting, deadly voice.

I scowled at him, confusion racing through me as Mama gasped, her fingers tightening on my shoulder. Then she was on her knees suddenly next to me, pressing her forehead to the rough wood of the floor.

"You are not Papa," I said bluntly.

"My Lord," Mama said in a shaking voice. "Forgive her. She does not know."

The man ignored her, his eyes burning into mine and there was a sharp pain under my ear. I watched as he brought that dark claw to his mouth, licking the droplet of red from it.

His head cocked to the side, surveying me. "Interesting," he mused.

Mama yelped as he wrapped that claw-tipped hand in her red curls and yanked her upright. "How long has she been like this?" He hissed; black eyes focused on her face. "I was not informed that she was not presenting anymore.

"Let Mama go," I shrieked, shoving at him. The backhand he gave me sent me crashing into our table, my back snapping one of the legs. I tasted blood and my head spun, but then Mama's hands were on me, lifting me to my feet. They shook slightly, but were firm on my shoulders and I peered up to her pale face, licking the blood from my split lip

"Since she was a couple of months old," Mama said in a trembling voice. "She is a good girl. Never any trouble. I give my report every quarter."

The man growled, low in his chest as he looked at me, the tip of a fang glinting as his lip curled.

"How dissapointing."

"I can keep her." Mama breathed. "If she isn't what you hoped for, I can keep her. She's no problem. My husband and I don't need any more coin from you. We can move away, and you won't have to think about her again I swear, My Lord."

The man's nose twitched as he looked towards the firepit. The black pot still hanging over the flames as the juices inside sizzled. His eyes narrowed. "Do you feed her what you were instructed, woman?"

Mama mewled softly, her hands bruising my shoulders. "I— we do, when we can get it for her. When we butcher a beast, she drinks her fill."

"Do I not give you coin, to ensure she is fed and clothed?" The man's voice was icy, and he took a step toward Mama.

A snarl rippled up my throat, but Mama's hands gripped even harder in warning.

"I appreciate everything you give us." Mama's voice was barely a whisper. "I make it stretch as best I can, I brought beasts to breed to try make it stretch further, but market prices have risen. My husband has taken work away to bring more money in, but we still cannot afford to keep her diet as rich as you asked."

"It was not a request," the man said coldly. "It was an order from your Lord. People have died for less, woman."

Mama shook behind me but didn't say anything.

He cocked his head again, eyeing me as I glared up at him.

"I wonder," he mused, running the tip of his claw along his chin.

I didn't even see him move. A cold hand closed around my throat, and I was jerked into the air.

Mama screamed as pain blossomed across my shoulder and I realised, shock dulling my mind, that the man had sunk his fangs into it with a low snarl. I grunted as he dropped me to the floor, my knees barking on the rough wood. I was panting in fear, looking round wildly for Mama as he eyed me curiously.

Mama was running to me. I don't know how we ended up across the room. I stumbled to my feet, opening my arms for her to pick me up, sobs tearing at my throat.

He stepped in front of her, his hand slashing across her face and I started screaming as blood sprayed.

She was close enough to me that warm droplets hit my face, my neck, and my outstretched hands.

"*Mama!*" I screamed as he stood over her. But his attention was focused on me, not her.

I scrabbled across the floor to her. She had a hand to the wound across her cheek and neck, blood dripping from between her fingers, but she tucked me against her body, her arm tight around me, her fingers gripping my dress, holding me away from him.

"Please," she moaned, beseeching him.

I watched him lift a booted foot and bared my teeth at him, waiting for the pain as he sent it into my stomach. But he smiled at me, a cruel, mirthless smile and stomped it down on Mama's ankle.

There was a dull crack. Mama convulsed, no sound coming from her, as her mouth opened in a silent scream, her fingers loosening on my dress.

Silence filled my head. That calm, hollow rage that had taken me before. Mama always held me when it happened, covered my face with kisses and sang to me until it left. But Mama couldn't hold me right now. Mama couldn't sing because she was screaming in pain, and this man was hurting her.

This man was going to die.

A dull pain ached in my gums, blood filling my mouth as my canines lengthened. Pain shot through my fingers as my claws sunk into the wood of the floor beneath me. I snarled at him, dark rage filling me as I struck. I sunk my claws into his chest, ripping myself up his body, lunging for his neck, ready to rip his throat out with my teeth. My teeth snapped together painfully in the air where warm flesh had been moments before. His hand closing around my throat again. It squeezed, lights entering into the corners of my suddenly sharp vision as his face appeared inches from mine.

He had a satisfied look on his face, ignoring my claws that were sunk deep into his wrist.

"Well, there you are," he said. His voice low. He pulled something out of his pocket, throwing it to Mama who cried softly on the ground. It thunked heavily onto the floor next to her, as a second followed a moment later.

"There is double there. See you do not disobey my instruction again, or she will get a new *Mama.*" He hissed.

Blackness was creeping over my vision as his hand tightened around my throat. My arms were too heavy to hold up. The last thing I heard before I slipped into unconsciousness was Mama's sobbed reply.

"Please. Please don't take her from me."

CHAPTER THREE

Age ten

"Papa!" I squealed, running towards him as the bells from our mule, Jak, announced his arrival. He chuckled, reaching a hand down and hauling me up into the saddle with him by my belt.

"You are almost too big to lift you up now, love," he teased, pinching my nose. "Did you have a good birthday last week?"

I nodded, burying my face into his shirt and wrapping my arms as far as they could go around him, which wasn't far. He smelled of camp smoke, mint, and of the balm Mama made him for his cough.

"Gosh, our little Lyrik, nine already!" He exclaimed, shaking his head.

I giggled as he slipped off the mule, holding his arms out for me. "I'm ten now, Papa," I laughed, grinning up at him as he put me down.

He peered down at me, resting a hand on my head and pretending to measure me.

"Naaahhh," he teased. "Little midget like you can't be ten!" He flipped open one of his saddlebags and reached into it, pulling out a cloth-wrapped bundle and winking at me. "Got you something."

I unwrapped it as he set about untying the line of goats that were tethered to the mule, cursing at the animals under his breath as they half dragged him across the yard, blatting and mumbling amongst themselves.

It was a beautiful, thick, dark green cloak, a metal clasp at the neck and a new pair of sturdy black boots.

"Oh, Papa, I love them," I breathed, brushing my hand across the soft material of the cloak.

"That's nice, love, come 'ere an grab one of these blasted creatures would you?"

I giggled, putting down my new gifts and running to him. I took the largest of the goats, tugging it into the goat barn easily and trotting back out to grab another from him, throwing down some fresh hay for them as well.

"Those two are in kid," he said, pointing his chin to the two contained. "This'un isn't, so we will have her for supper. Hungry, my girl?"

"Yes!" I exclaimed. "Do you need help butchering?"

"Nah, love, but I will come to say hello to Mama before I start."

We wandered back towards the house, his huge hand resting on my nape, engulfing almost the whole width of my shoulders and paused to grab one of his bags before heading into the house.

Mama was kneeding dough at the kitchen table, a streak of flour across one cheek.

"Hello, darling," Papa said, in that voice, he reserved especially for her.

"Well, hello there, handsome," Mama smiled, her face tired, but happy. She reached for her cane, wincing as she stood up and limped to him. Her ankle had never healed properly, and after a day's work, it always pained her. By evening she could usually barely stand on it, even with her cane.

I cringed as Papa kissed Mama, making a sound of disgust as

I went to the fire and put some water on to boil. "Gross."

Mama laughed behind me. "Enough of that, young lady. Why don't you go fetch in the rest of Papa's bags for him."

I rolled my eyes, holding my hand up to my face so I didn't have to watch them as I ran back outside to grab the rest of his pack bags. He had been gone two months this time. It was getting longer and longer. But he always made sure he was back for the quarterly reports. That man had not been back since, though my hatred for him grew every day, watching the pain Mama hid from her ruined ankle. By the time Papa returned home and Mama's ankle was half healed and couldn't be properly set.

I still had nightmares about that day. Mama's screams and his black eyes burning into me, waking me in the middle of the night to hover in my restless mind, mocking me for not being able to stop him.

I finished lugging the bags into the house as Papa headed outside to deal with the goat, chucking me under the chin as he passed, and I batted his hand away with a giggle.

Mama was sitting back in her chair, her leg up on a stool and was sniffing the contents of a jar, looking blissful.

"Here, Lyrik, have a sniff of what Papa brought me. Tea! Real tea!"

I obligingly sniffed it and promptly exploded into sneezes, Mama barely snatching the jar back before I blew it all over the cottage. She chuckled, placing it back on the table and pulling out a pile of rolled linen bandages from the bag Papa left behind.

"Papa brought these, too," she said, her face sobering slightly. I need you to wear them, Lyrik, as we discussed."

I squinted at them. "How do I do that?"

She crooked a finger at me. "Here, whip your shirt off, I will teach you."

The warmth of the fire heated the skin of my back as I stood between her knees and she wrapped one of the lengths of cloth tightly around my chest, tucking the end in under my arm. It was tight and scratchy, and I hated it.

"Mama it's horrible," I groused, bending dramatically one way and then the other. "It's too tight."

"I know, love, but you need to keep it on, even when you sleep."

"But why?" I whined, scratching my ribs.

Mama's face tightened slightly. "Because you are getting older, your body is going to start changing soon, and we can't let anyone see that. Better to get used to it now, than when you need it."

"Uuuuuuuugh!" I peered down at my chest and poked the barely-there breasts that had begun to appear. "Stupid things."

Papa came in later, red to the elbows, putting a pot of neatly cubed meat in front of Mama. She set about cooking, and I listened to the sounds of Papa washing his hands, his heavy footsteps ambling over to where I sat in front of the fireplace, scowling into the flames.

He nudged my knee with his boot. "What crawled up your ass, Midge?" He chuckled, handing me a pewter jug. It was filled to the brim with rich, dark blood, still warm. I stuck a finger down my bandages under my shirt, snapping the fabric loudly against my skin and giving Mama a dark look.

"Oh, right. Wimmin stuff." Papa huffed. "Drink up before it gets cold, leave some for later. You will be sick if you down it all."

I glared at the jug in my hands, sticking a finger in it and licking it clean. It tasted delicious, its soft undertones of spicy flavours sticking to my tastebuds, and I hummed in appreciation, taking long draws of the warm, thick liquid. It pooled in my belly, sending heat through me, a pleasant warm glow that spread out to my limbs.

A hand wrapped around mine, pulling the jug from my lips as I felt my belly begin to fill and I tightened my grip, giving a warning growl. My body wanted more; I was not ready to stop feeding.

"Midge. That's enough." Papa's voice was stern, and I jumped slightly. He never raised his voice to me. I let go of the jug, looking up at him sheepishly as I wiped my mouth on the back of my hand. "Sorry, Papa."

"It's ok, love," he soothed, taking my hand and peering at my fingers. "Good girl, you kept them in."

I ran my tongue over my teeth, checking them too, and winced as I cut it on the sharp points of my fangs that had slipped down and instantly felt disappointed with myself.

Papa noticed and ruffled my hair gently. "It's ok, you're getting there, Midge. You would have near bitten my hand off if I had tried stopping you mid-feed a few years back. Do you still want some of Mama's stew?"

I shook my head, yawning. "I'm full. Can I have a story though?"

Papa chuckled softly, moving to his large chair next to the fire and slumping into it, patting his knee. "Come on then, Midget. While you still fit on my lap."

Chapter Four

Age fourteen

I woke to the sound of Mama murmuring to Papa. I could tell she was upset by the tone of her voice.

They had moved me up into the loft not long after my twelfth birthday, Papa saying I needed more privacy now. I liked it up there. It was warm and cosy, and I had a little window I could see out of and watch the stars at night.

I half-heartedly tried to listen to what Mama was saying, my ears perking up as I heard my name a couple of times, but I couldn't make out any words.

Mama had been quiet recently, and even Papa had been spending less time away from home, pushing out his trips until he *had* to go.

The quarterly report was coming any day now. I knew Mama was stressing about it. I hated that it was because of me.

They sat me down last year and told me of my birth… and who my sire was. I had lost control of myself for a week afterwards, letting the emptiness take over so I didn't have to feel the anger and guilt that burned through me. Even now, every time I looked at Mama, limping heavily as she went about her day, my heart hurt for the pain I had inadvertently brought upon her.

Mama had eventually gotten through that numbness. Finding me in the woods after I had killed and fed on a pack of wolves, sitting with me until I gradually let myself slip back. Papa had gone white with shock as we walked up to the cottage, both of us covered in gore and blood, and Mama limping so heavily I was nearly carrying her, but neither of us were hurt.

I had known I was different. For one, Mama had beautiful red hair that shone like fire. Papa had olive skin and dark hair like many of the people in Mircia, except for the Drayvn who all had fair skin with their dark hair. My golden blonde hair was unusual in these lands, harking to neither Drayvn nor Mircian lineage. It had come from my birth mother, who I knew nothing of.

The other fact made abundantly clear was that Mama and Papa were not Drayvn— and I was. Or at least, I was when I lost my grip on myself.

I wriggled on the straw of my mattress, running a finger along the bindings across my chest. I had a sore on my ribs on one side and it itched infernally. I longed to remove it and take a massive, rib-cracking breath in, but Mama panicked every time I took it off— even just to bathe. I ran my hand over my chest, feeling the tender mounds of my small breasts beneath and sent a prayer to the Gods they wouldn't get any bigger. The Gods knew Mama would just wrap me tighter.

I sighed, my stomach hollow and I ran a hand through my hair, untangling it as I worked up to rising. My bed was so cosy and the air, when I had slipped a testing foot out of the sheets, was cool.

Papa was warming my breakfast over the fire as I climbed down my rickety ladder, Mama's tea bubbling next to it.

"Mornin›, Midge," he rumbled, pouring the warmed steer blood into a large mug and nudging it across the table to me.

"Drink up, love, I would say quarter report is this week."

I had learned that Mama had tried to hide my Drayvn side at first, in the hopes my sire would reject me as he had his other female offspring, but the night he had arrived himself to check on me had changed that entirely.

"Lyrik, I need you to listen carefully to me."

The blood cooled in my throat suddenly, and I nearly choked on it. Papa never called me by my name unless it was serious.

"You are nearly fifteen, love," Papa said gently. "Mama thinks your sire will consider you mature anytime now. We have been looking at where we can take you that is safe, and I think I may have found somewhere. But we will need to leave straight after the report. That will be the best time to do it."

I swallowed hard. The blood suddenly sticky in my throat. "Where?"

"Papa found a man who will hide us in cargo leaving for Calibyre," Mama said, limping out of her room to join us at the table. She took the cup of tea Papa offered her, leaning into him to take the weight off her ankle, and gave me a smile full of tenderness and love. "It will be safe for us all there; we just need to get out of Mircia first.

"But Papa said it was suicide to run away from him," I said, panic beginning to rise in me. "What if they come after us and they hurt you again, Mama?" There was a grinding noise, and I looked down to see my claws had slipped out and were embedded deep into the splintered wood of the table.

"Don't lose yourself, love." Mama leaned forward, putting a warm hand over mine, her thumb stroking the back of my hand. "Deep breaths."

I did as I was told, taking a deep, steadying breath in, and felt the roiling push in my blood recede slightly.

"There's my girl," Mama soothed, lifting my fingers to her lips and kissing the knuckles. "It is dangerous," she continued, keeping my hand wrapped in hers. "But we are doing this together. I'm not letting him take you from us."

"What if I just go when he tells me to," I ask, fear still clutching at my stomach. "And then I can come back and visit all the time. And then it's not putting you and Papa in danger, Mama?"

"No." The abruptness of Mama's words made me blink in surprise. "No." she softened her voice, but I could feel a tremor in her hands. "What they do to women up there—what I have seen." She shook her head. "No daughter of mine will be a pawn of the Drayvn."

"But, Mama, *I'm* Drayvn," I argued. "Maybe it will be different for m—"

"No, Lyrik." Mama cut me off. "You are far, far more than a Drayvn. Your heart is nothing like those *males*. You are good and kind. You are more than your blood. You are *our* daughter, and we swore we would keep you safe. So, this is how we do it."

Papa patted Mama on the back gently, giving me a *'don't argue with your mother'* look over her shoulder.

"Ok, Mama," I said. Though fear had now settled hard and cold in my guts. "Should I pack?"

"No," Papa said. "We cannot let them see we are thinking of leaving. My trips away have been good cover as I have searched, but if they see what we are planning, it could be disastrous. When we go, we leave everything behind. Just as if we were going to the market or visiting a friend."

A Drayvn male arrived three days later for the report. His cold, emotionless eyes raked over me as I stood, feeling like a prize heifer at a sale in our small cottage.

"You are feeding regularly?" He asked, his voice cutting through the warmth of our cozy home. I had seen this one before.

He stood taller than most, nearly the same height as Papa, who was currently glowering at him from the hearth.

"Yes," I bit out, feeling my fangs begin to lengthen as I eyed the man's neck, visions of sinking my teeth into it slipping unbidden into my mind.

His lip curled as he raked his eyes insolently up my body, lingering on my chest. I wore a loose shirt, but even with the wrappings, my breast were beginning to show through where the fabric clung to me.

"You are abnormally small for a Drayvn. Are these two withholding food to push out your maturing?" He cocked his head at Mama and Papa, and my temper surged.

"You are abnormally thick for one," I bit back before I could catch myself. "My *sire* isn't exactly tall either."

Mama made a small choking sound, her hand going to her throat, and she stared at me with wide eyes, shaking her head ever so slightly.

The Drayvn smiled a cruel smile and took a step towards me. I didn't flinch as he raised a hand, expecting a blow, but he simply ran a clawed finger lightly down the side of my face, his black eyes burning into mine. He ran the finger down, tracing over my lip and then down over the fabric of my shirt, pausing between my breasts. He pushed his claw in, and I heard the small pop as it went through the cotton, the blunt pressure as it pushed against my skin, protected by the layers of my bindings.

Papa made a move to my right, and I glared at him, stopping him in his tracks. He had a face like thunder, his rage honed in on the Drayvn in front of me.

The Drayvn tutted softly as he drew the finger back and glanced at it, his smile turning my spine to ice.

"Have you bled yet?" He asked, nonchalantly.

I felt my cheeks warm in outrage and embarrassment. "N-no," I stuttered, instantly furious at my lack of control over myself.

"Hmmm," the Drayvn hummed, raising a brow at me. "Teeth."

I bared my fangs at him, snarling low in my throat, and he gave me a mirthless laugh in return.

He pulled a pouch from the depths of his cloak, dropping it onto the table with a *thunk*, not even acknowledging Mama or Papa as he did. "I will see you soon then," he said, his voice a low purr as he made a mocking bow and headed towards the exit. "And stop wearing those ridiculous binders. Makes me think you are hiding something."

CHAPTER FIVE

"Just leave it, love, we can buy new books in Calibyre," Papa said, shoving a few items into a bag as mum wrapped the food up into another.

"But it's the one you wrote me," I pleaded, running my hand across the leather binding of the book. It was the most precious thing I owned. Papa had given it to me on my seventh birthday after tediously writing all my favourite stories onto paper he had collected on his travels and binding them for me for Mama to read to me whenever he was away.

Papa's face softened as he looked at me. "I think it's time for an upgrade don't you think?" He winked. "You can pick all your favourites when we get there, and I will make you one so thick you won't be able to lift it."

I looked down at my book and nodded, trying to swallow the disappointment. I knew it was silly, being so caught up on a book when we were leaving everything behind. But this had been my comfort on so many nights. I climbed my ladder one last time and tucked my book into my bed, hoping that whoever took the house over, once it was realised as abandoned, had a child who would enjoy it as much as I had.

Mama held my cloak open for me as I jumped back down, landing soundlessly on the floor. It was still its beautiful dark green, the metal clasp glinting duly at the neck, but it was threadbare at the hem now, coming to mid-calf rather than trailing on the floor as it had. I fingered the small hole in the hem from where the fireplace had spat an ember at me while I watched Papa soundlessly throw all of the remaining feed down for the goats and refilled all of the troughs. It would be enough, we had visitors usually once a week or so to swap eggs and vegetables for the milk and meat we had, and they would soon realise we had left.

Mama cut the bells off of Jak, hushing him as he brayed softly.

The Drayvn had spooked them badly last night. Mama said she had a bad feeling about him, and Papa had pushed forward the plans by a week, saying we would leave immediately. If we got to the docks early, it would be easier to hide in the large city, which was two-weeks ride from my sire's castle, than it would be here.

My entire being crackled with excitement and nerves. I had never been further than the market, and Papa had told me all about the arid landscape of Calibyre, its deserts and beautiful tropical forests full of birds and beasts that even he struggled to describe.

Papa lifted Mama onto Jak, tucking her dress in around her legs, and giving her a smile. He held his arms out for me next, but I shook my head, stating I would walk with him instead.

I looked back over my shoulder as we rounded the bend away from our cottage. Mama had left the fire going in the hearth and smoke curled from its lopsided chimney. The threadbare curtains were drawn and in the evening light, a soft glow filtered through the thin fabric. It looked as it always had, of comfort and home. I kept my face away from Papa as a hot tear ran down my cheek to drip onto the cold ground as we walked.

The snow hadn't yet begun to fall, the ground hard enough not to leave tracks, but nights were frigid. Papa had decided we would travel through the nights, the movement keeping us warm and then rest during the days where— if followed— travellers would be more noticed. I didn't mind, I liked the night, and we passed the next few nights making pictures from the stars, Mama pointing out constellations and teaching us their names.

Papa's cough was worse in the cold air, and the familiar scent of the herbal balm Mama slathered over him wrapped around me as I walked next to him. He held my hand sometimes, swinging my arm as we walked. I was far too old to be holding my Papa's hand, but I liked it, his huge palm engulfing my hand *and* wrist made me feel younger than I was, reminding me of the days when it was just me, Mama and Papa and I didn't know the severity of my situation.

Mama began to relax close to the fourth day. The strained lines of her face softened, and her easy smile returned. She even sang for us, coaxing me to join her. She always loved it when I sang for her, saying my voice was almost as beautiful as my temper was devastating.

I just like watching Papa as she sang. The way he looked at Mama always made my heart feel warm.

We reached a small settlement on the fifth day. Papa left Mama and me in the woods to go in and make some enquiries. He came back not long later to tell us he had paid a local farmer to be able to stay in his barn. There was feed for Jak, and we could rest the day out of the sun. The barn was nothing special, a few pens which Papa led Jak into, a loft up high that had sacks of feed loaded in and huge piles of hay in the back part.

Papa lay a couple of blankets down on these and both Mama

and I collapsed into them, exhausted and very grateful for somewhere soft to sleep.

I woke as the sun was low in the sky, a beam of dusky light was shining through a crack in the barn wall, landing on my face. I gazed at it a while, dust particles swirling lazily through the shaft of light and turned my head, rustling against my bed of straw to see Mama and Papa, curled together in their own nest.

Mam's head was on Papa's broad chest, his arm around her shoulders and his free hand was twined with hers on his chest, resting over his heart.

There was a skin of water and a cloth-wrapped bundle next to my bed and I flicked the wrapping open with my finger curiously. A thick slice of travel cake lay inside, and I hummed appreciatively, sitting up and tucking into it, crumbs going everywhere as I munched happily.

Mama chuckled sleepily and I grinned at her, washing a mouthful of the fruity mess down with water and nearly choking on it.

"My Gods, you feral little creature," Mama teased, eyeing me over Papa's chest. "Look at you, hay sticking out your hair, crumbs everywhere and eating like I haven't fed you in months."

I stuck my cake-covered tongue out at her, and she winced, looking slightly disgusted.

Papa cracked an eye open, gazing blearily at me. "Go give Jak some fresh water, Midge, since you are so alarmingly awake and then pop over to the farmhouse, I paid for some bread when we got here, and they said it would be ready before we left."

I nodded, popping the last of my cake in my mouth, wiping my hands on the straw and getting uncertainly to my feet in the springy hay.

Papa gathered Mama to him, nuzzling her neck and murmuring to her.

"Gross," I muttered, brushing hay off my clothes.

Papa stuck his foot out of bed as I passed, hooking my ankle and chuckling darkly as I tumbled into the soft hay at their feet.

"Life is not worth living without love, young Midge. Remember that."

"Do you have to be so…" I waved my hand at them, my lips curling in disgust as I staggered to my feet again, throwing a handful of hay at them. "You about it?"

Papa raised his brow at me and then launched onto Mam, kissing her loudly as she giggled.

"Ugh," I groaned, covering my eyes and stumbling over to Jaks› pen. "Gods save me."

I filled Jaks' trough from the barrels of water next to the pens, giving his wiry head a quick scratch before blinking out into the evening sun.

The farmhouse we had stopped at stood a couple of paddocks over nestled in a copse of trees, I could just see the smoke from the fire curling up through the branches.

"I'm going now!" I called, shoving my feet into my boots.

The farmer's wife was a young, gifted earth Sylvyn called Ezrah. She was busily tending her vegetable garden as I arrived, and let me watch, entranced for a while as she coaxed small plants out of the freshly tilled earth. They unfurled under her hand, the small, fresh leaves spreading like flowers in neat little rows.

"The bread came out of the oven not long past— Midge? Was it?" she said, her voice as pretty as her face was. "Come inside while I wrap it for you, I have squeezed orange juice as well if you would like some?"

I nodded, not bothering to correct the nickname Papa had for me, following her into the simple little cottage and sipping on the cup of tart orange juice she gave me while I watched her work. There were potted plants all through the cottage, beautiful flowers of all different colours and vines growing from others, curling across the rafter with fragrant white blossoms on them.

"Here you go," she said, handing me three paper-wrapped loaves, her long brown hair falling over her shoulder. They were still warm and the heat of them seeped through the front of my shirt as I cradled them to my chest.

"Your da already paid, so no need for that," she smiled. She passed me a fourth, smaller loaf, the size of my fist, one edge slightly blackened. "This one fell in the fire, so you can have it for free."

"Thank you," I replied, tucking the last under my chin as I made my way to the door.

I walked back along the dirt path, taking small bites of the loaf and watching the birds follow me from tree limb to tree limb. I whistled back some of their tunes to them, smiling as they hopped nearer and I broke off some of the blackened bread crust, throwing it for them.

I stomped my feet dramatically as I neared the barn again. Walking as heavy as a drunk sailor. "I'm baaaaaaack," I called, rolling my eyes to myself. "You need to stop kissing now."

There was a scuffle against hay, and I waited a moment, walking slowly backwards up to the entrance. "The bread is good," I called again, giving them *ample* time to stop whatever they were doing. "The lady, Ezrah, gave me an extra one for free. But I ate some of it."

There was a grunt from behind me and I sighed, turning slowly. "Ok, I gave you plenty of warn—"

My eye fell on the horse, tied to the far side of the barn, just as I saw the Drayvn, his clawed hand around Mam's throat, her body dangling as his black, emotionless eyes fixed on me.

CHAPTER SIX

"I said I would see you again soon." His voice was casual as if he had seen me at the market and stopped to say hello.

My loaves thunked to the ground, my arms turning to lead weights at my sides. "No, don't," I whispered. Terror was clutching at my mind, a cold, spreading weight through my stomach.

Mama was gasping, her hands pulling at the fingers wrapped around her neck.

"Put her down," I moaned, my eyes searching the barn for Papa. "Please, put her down."

The Drayvn's mouth quirked in a cruel smile. He lowered Mama until her toes brushed the ground, taunting her as she gasped and dragged in strangled breaths.

"Lyrik, run!" she bit out before he cut her off again with a cruel squeeze.

I stumbled forward, reaching for her, and the Drayvn dragged her backwards a step. The movement turned them side-on to me, letting me see further back into the barn.

I saw him then, ice curling in my veins.

Blood pooled on the floor under his large body, a knife still clutched in his fingers and his eyes, those eyes that had looked at me with such love just moments before, were staring up at the roof. Unseeing.

I don't know when I started screaming, but suddenly I was kneeling in his warm blood, my hands trying to hold the jagged mess of his neck closed, pleading with him to get up.

"Papa," I heard myself say, over and over again, as if I were looking down on myself.

I shook his shoulder, willing him to be ok. "Papa please," I begged. But the blood had stopped running through my fingers. There was no steady thump under my hand. Papa was gone.

Claws descended from my fingers, a low snarl ripping from my throat as I turned my head, glaring at the Drayvn, still holding Mama.

"Such a touching sight," he mocked, dipping his head to sniff Mama's hair. "And such a pretty little flower, so *delicious*," he murmured. "Even if a bit broken." He kicked her maimed ankle, drawing a pained cry from her.

"Get away from her," I snarled, my fangs sliding out as I snarled at him. I kept the hollowness at bay, not letting it take over completely. "Put. Her. Down."

The Drayvn smiled coldly. "I don't think I will."

He released her neck slightly, and Mama took a shuddering breath, sobbing as she looked at Papa with heartbroken eyes. "Lyrik, please," she whispered. "Please run."

The pressure in my head was growing, the urge to descend into the silence that loomed up in my blood almost overwhelming and I snarled again, stalking towards them. He was my prey, and I was going to enjoy killing him."

"Lyrik, don't lose yourself," Mama pleaded, her eyes filling with tears as she reached a hand for me. It hovered in the space between us. Reaching for me like they had an immeasurable number of times in my life. "I love you. Just breathe and stay with me."

My vision cleared slightly, and I stepped towards her hand, reaching to take it.

"But that's exactly what we want," the Drayvn said coldly. And then his hand moved viciously across Mama's neck.

I watched as utter emotionless calm flooded through me when Mama's body hit the floor, her arm still outstretched to me, those beautiful eyes still looking at me, filled with love.

Stay with me. The words echoed in my mind... but she was gone, and there was nothing left for me to clutch to now, nothing to stop the hollowness that had opened like a void in my chest, swallowing everything.

I tilted my head, looking up at the Drayvn as a rumbling snarl started up my chest, my body dropping into a crouch. And then I struck.

My fangs ripped into his flesh, hitting bone in his arm and he roared.

I dully felt the impact as his fist cracked against my jaw, dislodging me. I released my grip but clawed at him, teeth snapping as I tried to sink them into his neck, trying to rip the life from him as he had just done to the only people I had left in the world.

My body crashed against one of the pens. I vaguely heard Jak's frantic bray before I was on the Drayvn again, claws sinking deep into anything I could get to. I was ripping and tearing at him. Blood coated my hands and dripped down my chin. Warm rivulets of it soaked the front of my shirt. His blood— I wanted all of it.

He had stopped taunting me as he lashed. Where he grasped my arm, I struck with the other. Where he bit, I drove my knee into his chest. I was death, and I wanted his. It was the only thing I cared about.

He grunted as I twisted, my fangs sinking deep into his neck finally. A spurt of warm blood down my throat let me know I had hit something vital. We went down, his claws slicing at my back and head as he tried to pull me from him, but I just bit deeper, drawing his blood into me with a low growl.

His thrashing grew weaker; his grip on me loosening as I snarled in satisfaction—when something suddenly moved next to me… then the world went black.

I awoke to pain. Fiery streaks of it across my scalp, my back, my legs, though it paled in comparison to the pain that was tearing at my heart.

I was slumped over the rump of a horse, its jolting strides making my head bob excruciatingly with every step. I reached to push the hair from my face, stuck uncomfortably to my skin, and realised my hands were bound with thick, course rope so tight that they had gone white.

"She's awake, Kalius." The voice came from somewhere behind us and I tried to lift my head, groaning as it pulled at wounds on my neck.

The horse stopped and the warmth that had been in front of me disappeared.

Boots entered my field of vision against the frozen ground and a hand wrapped painfully in my hair, yanking my head up to meet cold, black eyes.

"Can you speak?"

I spat in his face, watching with satisfaction as the glob slid down his cheek.

Then the world went black again.

The next time I woke, I was laid out close to a fire. My hands throbbed uncomfortably, and I was desperate to relieve my bladder. The thought of wetting myself on top of everything else was just too much to bear. I twisted, peering across the flames, looking for the men that had been around before.

There was no one here. I sat up, moaning in pain as whatever injuries I had on my back tugged and pulled. My head throbbed and my mouth was dry. Memories flooded back to me, and I was paralysed by the flood of anguish that gripped me. Mama's face burned into my memories the moment before her life had been taken from her. From me.

I rolled to my knees awkwardly, hissing as my bound hands took my weight, painful stabbing sensations coursing through them. Mercifully, my feet were untied and I stumbled as far away as the length of rope I was tethered with allowed, wriggling out of my pants and relieving myself at the edge of the camp.

Getting them back on was a challenge, my hands were useless, all feeling in them gone as I struggled to grasp and draw them back up again.

My shirt was caked in blood. Papa's blood covered my pants, and I tried not to look at them. It just brought back his face, sightless and muted.

Tears ran down my cheeks as I looked around the simple camp. I had been tied to a tree on the far side of the horses. Two of them were hobbled away from the fire. The rope snapped tight just before I could reach the flames, the same as it did when I attempted to reach any of the bags that were stacked on its other side

I hissed in frustration, turning back to the tree and peering at the knot. I couldn't even begin to undo it with my hands, as numb as they were. I tried reaching it with my teeth, but even stretching on my toes I couldn't get to it.

There was a quiet laugh from behind me and I spun, tripping over a root and landing heavily on my rear. I gasped as the wounds on my back and sides flared with pain, feeling one open, blood trickling down my spine.

The Drayvn from before, Kalias, was surveying me across the flames.

"Are you hungry?" he asked, as if this was just another day for him. I don't know why that simple question ignited such a fire in me, but it did, simmering in my chest. I didn't answer, glaring at him instead.

"Thirsty then?" he tried again.

I was, desperately, but I was not telling him that.

He grunted, turning away from me and sitting down on a fallen log.

I watched him warily, my eyes skirting the surrounding forest for the owner of the other horse.

"Where are you taking me?" I bit out.

"To your sire." was the simple reply.

I bared my teeth at him. "Let me go."

He ignored me.

I swore at him, using the filthiest words I had ever heard Papa use.

He still ignored me.

"I see she woke up." A dry voice said from the shadows under the trees.

I recognised the voice as the one I had heard earlier and studied him as he stepped into the light cast by the fire. He was not Drayvn, though the hard angles of his face were nearly as unforgiving as Drayvn features. They made him look older than I thought at first glance, which was confirmed when he turned and I saw his ears had indeed begun to tip into the Sylvyn point, not the long tips Mama and Papa had, but enough to show he was past his late twenties. His long dark hair was shaved on the sides, the top section braided into a long plait tucked into the back of his cloak.

He had a hare slung over a shoulder, a bow in his hand, and he dropped the former with a thud next to the fire.

"Blood is still warm if you want it?" He said casually to Kalias, his blade hovering under the hare's neck.

Kalias lip curled in disgust. "You can keep your rodent blood, Darius, I've already fed."

Darius huffed softly. "Nice of you to share." He pointed his knife at me. "What about you, little one, do you want it?"

I shook my head, scowling at him.

He shrugged, turning back to his kill and busied himself preparing it, making quick work of the skinning and butchering. It was skewered on sharpened sticks and sizzling over the flames in no time.

My stomach grumbled as the smell of the cooking meat wafted to me. I had retreated to the tree, my back against its rough surface and my arms awkwardly crossed to avoid touching the stiff, blood-caked fabric of my pants. It felt like a betrayal. How could my body hunger? How could I be sitting here breathing, while Mama and Papa couldn't?

I was spiralling back into my misery when Darius nudged my foot with his boot. I felt my lip draw back in a snarl, the vibration of it rattling in my chest.

"None of that," Darius said lightheartedly. "You need to eat something; you took a good few injuries back there and we won't get to the healers for another couple of days." He held a plate out to me, and my stomach clenched painfully in response to the scent of the meat.

He leaned down, holding it closer.

I lashed out, slapping the plate out of his hand and sending the meat and plate flying.

Darius raised a brow at the mess on the floor. "Well, that was uncalled for," he sighed. "I am not your enemy, Lyrik."

"You are all my enemy." I hissed at him.

"Give her water and leave her be. She deserves to suffer a while after the damage she did to Andrei," Kalias muttered from his seat.

It unnerved me, watching him. I had not had the chance to observe Drayvn as I did now. I had only seen them during the visits to our cottage. At rest they sat preternaturally still, it reminded me of the vipers Papa warned me about whenever we walked through the forests. Coiled. Watching. Ready to strike at all times.

"Andrei deserved to be taken down a peg," Darius said. "Look at her, she's five-foot-nothing and ripped half his throat out like butter. She would have had him if we hadn't arrived."

This was news to me. Anger curled in my guts as his face floated into my memories. His cruel, unforgiving eyes as he murdered Mama. Now I had a name. Andrei, and he was alive.

It was at that moment every plan for escape, every thought I had tried to scrape together on how to get away from these men evaporated, a new goal firmly settling into my mind. I was going to let these men take me back to my sire's castle. I would find Andrei, and I would make him feel every single ounce of pain Mama and Papa had felt three times over before I killed him.

CHAPTER SEVEN

I didn't sleep that night. I couldn't if I had tried. Even with vengeance now whispering in my ear, my heart hurt so badly that I had given in to my tears as darkest night had shielded me from my captor's view. It felt like a wound, so deep in my chest that there were moments I thought my heart might actually be bleeding.

The lure of letting myself slip into the muted calm of my Drayvn blood was unbearable, but I fought it with every breath. If I gave in to it, my priorities would shift. Logical thought would replace the desperate need my broken heart had for vengeance. Drayvn-Lyrik would find a means of escape. I did not want to escape; they were taking me right to the person I wanted.

I was trying to rub life back into my aching, numb hands as daybreak hit, hissing at the stabbing pain in my fingers.

Kalias came to loom over me, his face unreadable and dropped a bundle of fabric next to me.

"You reek. Change."

Darius snorted from where he was packing his bedroll, the leather tie between his teeth.

"Such a conversationalist you are, Kalias," he mouthed around it. He glanced at me. "She's gonna struggle to do that without hands."

Kalias narrowed his eyes at me and then grabbed me by the front of my ruined shirt, hauling me to my feet.

I snapped at him as one hand fisted the fabric of my pants, trying to yank them down, kicking him hard in the shin. Don't fucking touch me," I snarled.

Papa would have tanned my ass for talking like that. Papa wasn't here anymore.

"*Kallliiaaas*," Darius drawled, an exasperated look on his face. "How are you going to get the shirt on her? Chuck it over her head and leave her arms inside? Her hands are going blue, they will drop off if you try to leave them that tight the whole way back. Lord Vasilica will be none too pleased if his fourteen-year investment comes back missing crucial parts of her anatomy. Just untie her."

Kalias shook me until my teeth rattled, stars flickering in my vision. "Be still," he growled. He turned to Darius, "You saw what she did to Andrei, you think she won't do the same to you?"

Darius rolled his eyes, getting up and sauntering to us, pulling a wicked-looking blade from his belt and pointing it at the base of my neck. "Happy?" He said, cocking his head to Kalias and giving him a sweet smile. "Or... whatever you lot feel? Satisfied? Dead inside? Slightly *less* dead inside?"

Kalias just narrowed his eyes at him, before turning his attention back to me. "Change," he said threateningly before moving back to his belongings.

Darius grinned at me, then slipped the knife between my hands, cutting the rope there.

Warmth pooled through my hands; white-hot stabs of pain ran into my fingers as the blood rushed back into my hands. I gasped, trying to clench my fingers in an effort to help the process along.

It took a while to fumble myself into the clothes, my cheeks heating as Darius talked the whole time, his knife tip brushing my neck as he did. It was the first time I had ever been grateful for my binders, shielding my body from their view. The clothes swamped me. The shirt, which must have been one of theirs, fell past my knees. And the pants they had given me wouldn't even come close to staying up.

Darius wrinkled his nose as he surveyed me, the shirt tucked in, the waistband of the pants wadded in my fist, trying to hold them up.

"Gods, girl. Lose the pants, the shirt is as good as a dress on you anyway."

I looked down in dismay, stepping out of the pants reluctantly and jumping as he leaned down, deftly cutting a length of the rope off and wrapping it like a belt around my stomach. It cinched the shirt in at the waist, making it less sack-like and letting me move easier. It still came to my knees, the bulky boots Mama had picked up for me sticking out the bottom.

The course rope slid around my neck as Darius retied it there, knotting it efficiently with an intricate-looking knot as he held his knife between his teeth.

"Now," he said, taking his knife and waving the tip in front of my face. "Don't be doing anything stupid now, or Kalias over there will most likely hogtie you to the back of his horse for the rest of this trip. Got it?"

I nodded sullenly, still rubbing my exsanguinated hands together.

I rode with Darius in silence, permitted to sit in front of him rather than slumped over Kalias horse rump as I had been. I ignored his efforts at conversation, doggedly keeping my mind focused on my next movements, my plans, anything to avoid the chasm that was yawning wider and wider in my heart.

He gave up on the third day, slipping into silence broken only by the horse's thudding hooves and the birds that sang around us, oblivious to the horror of what had been done in this peaceful countryside.

I ate the food and drank the water they gave me. I slept when they told me to. I was a good little captive, a docile little snake that they were taking back to their hencoop.

On the fourth day, I began to recognise my surroundings, passing the far side of the small lake that the market bordered, its cold, dark water serene against the frigid backdrop.

The air had become bitterly cold, the only thing keeping me from frozen misery was my threadbare cloak and the warmth of Darius› body at my back. My feet ached with it though, and I hadn't felt my toes in days.

Kalias didn't feel the cold. No Drayvn did. Where Darius and I wrapped ourselves in our clothes, he rode ahead, stony face fixed on the path ahead, wearing only the light cotton shirt he had been in this whole time, black hair pulled back into a tight plait and cloak billowing out behind him.

I eyed the back of his head, daydreaming about how it would feel when my teeth crushed down on his spine.

My sire›s castle sat on the edge of a dense forest. The stronghold of the Drayvn of Mircia. I learned later this was but one of the properties he had over Mircia, but Corvin Castle was where his harem resided. It was the centre of his power, and the centre of the Drayvn hold over Mircia.

It was beautiful, its great rock walls and tile-capped turrets reaching proudly for the sky, hiding the monsters that lived within.

The only access to the entrance was a long, narrow bridge, wide enough to take a cart across it, or two horses abreast. I peered down the side as we rode along, the river in the canyon below a dark line twisting around the cliffs .

The great entrance doors ahead swung open as we neared, revealing a large cobbled courtyard, and striding towards us was my sire.

My stomach turned to ice as I watched the man, whose fangs I still bore the scars from, eye me. The last time I had looked upon his face, he had his hand around my throat and Mama was pleading on the floor behind us. He looked exactly the same, and I had to force myself not to spit at him, the image of Mama hobbling painfully every winter flashing through my mind.

"Daughter," he said in greeting as if my life had not been ripped apart under his orders.

"I am no daughter of yours," I said, my own tone as cold as his.

His brow raised slightly, his gaze sliding over me to Darius at my back. "Well done," he said casually.

Darius bowed his head to my sire as he dismounted, reaching to pull me off afterwards. I stumbled awkwardly as my feet hit the ground. They were numb and clumsy beneath me as I tried to take my weight on them.

"Andrei?" Kalias asked, from my other side as he dismounted, handing his horse to a groom.

"Fine," my sire said coldly, his eyes snapping back to me. "Though he learned a good lesson." He cocked his head, looking over me. "Shift," he said cooly, his eyes narrowing.

I glared back at him, my hands clenched at my sides and made myself stand motionless as he stepped towards me, his face inches from mine.

"I said, *shift.*"

"No," I hissed.

"I wouldn't push me, girl. You have caused trouble for me, not to mention the fact you damaged my son — your brother. There is only so much I will let slide before you reap the consequences of your actions."

His words settled over me like a layer of frost. *My brother. Andrei, the Drayvn that had murdered my family. I shared blood with him.* The thought turned my stomach, and I felt my lips twist with disgust.

"You have already taken everything I care about from me," I spat at him. My heart thundering in my ears. "I do not fear you."

His lips curled into that same smile he had given me so many years ago. Cold and calculating. "That's where you are wrong, daughter. There is still much I can take from you. And I will start with your obedience."

He snapped his fingers at two Drayvn standing behind him. "Take her to the north wing, tell Gheata to deal with her." His nose wrinkled as he ran his eyes ran over me. "She stinks of blood and farm animals. Inform Gheata I expect her in my offices tonight."

"Yes, father," the older of the men said, bowing.

Another brother. Another target.

CHAPTER EIGHT

The woman in front of me, Gheata, was beautiful. But her beauty didn't stretch to her eyes, which were as hard and cold as any of the Drayvn I had met so far.

She had long, dark hair that hung past her hips, the sides of it braided back and tied behind her head. She had fair skin and full lips, the picture of delicate beauty, but the strength in her hands as she hauled me off the floor where I was thrown, told me it was all a mask.

I had been deposited in what looked like a large living space. A large black marble fireplace dominated one wall, flanked on either side by carved statues of Druka, the dragons that roamed the mountains of Mircia. But the hearth was cold, no fire heating the room.

There were day couches in areas around the room, carpets of a deep, wine-red spread across the rock floor and women watched me from various activities with wary expressions on their faces. Two were pregnant, one so round she looked like she was about to burst was reclining on a couch, a thick blanket around her shoulders. Another, her stomach much smaller, leaned against a marble pillar, her hand pressed to her side, massaging the skin there.

Gheata dragged me across to a doorway, shoving me unceremoniously through it and pointing to a copper tub in the corner. "Take those clothes off and leave them in the corner. Servants will be up shortly to scrub that filth off you." She looked at me coldly. "I expected… more." Her gaze raked over me, narrowing on my face.

I shook her hand off my arm and nodded shortly, waiting until the door slammed behind her before I let myself relax and take in my surroundings. This was his harem. The women that bore his children. Where my mother had been up until my birth had killed her.

Servants arrived with hot water, even in the smaller space the air was so cold I gasped as I shrugged out of my makeshift dress. One of them gave me an odd look as they untied my bindings, the skin underneath was sensitive as they fell away. My feet protested cruelly at the sudden warmth as I stepped into the water making me gasp with the prickling pain of it.

It took three changes of water before it ran clear. I hadn't realised how much blood was still on me until the water turned a murky red as rough hands scrubbed at my hair. I was hauled out of the tub and dressed in a dark blue dress with a warm slip beneath it, two of the women tackling the tangled snarls of my hair with combs as a healer moved around me, treating the wounds that had softened in the water.

The clothes were better quality than anything I had ever owned, Mama would have had to use half of the quarterly coin to purchase them, and it felt wrong, this easy wealth after they had struggled so harshly.

Gheata emerged back into the room as they were just finishing, curling my still damp hair into a tight bun behind my head.

She looked over me, her face tight with dislike that seeped

from her in almost visible waves before she nodded shortly. "Acceptable," she said through tight lips.

I followed her out into the main room. The woman there before had vanished, the room eerily quiet as she pointed to a table. "Sit. Eat. I will be back soon to retrieve you."

I didn't bother arguing. I was tired and hungry, and the scent that was wafting from one of the pewter cups made my mouth water. Lambs blood, and it was fresh.

I was so engrossed in quenching the burning thirst in my throat that I didn't notice that one of the women had re-appeared in Gheata's absence. I noticed her as I lowered the cup, my stomach comfortably full for the first time in days. She was standing cautiously in a doorway, her eyes wary as they tracked the empty cup I slowly lowered, my tongue catching the droplet that had slipped down my lip.

"You look just like her," she said softly, offering me a small smile.

I froze, feeling as if the air had been sucked from my lungs.

Her brows pinched together slightly. "What is your name?"

"L—" My words caught in my throat, and I had to clear it twice before I could speak again. "Lyrik."

She looked pained for a moment, then nodded, a sad smile tugging at her lips.

"She would have liked that."

"You knew my mother?" my voice sounded hollow.

She nodded, a true smile brightening her face as her eyes unfocused lightly in memory. "Not for long. I arrived here not long before—" she broke off, hesitating. "Before your birth. She was kind to me though. She was... one of the only ones who wouldn't let Gheata order her around."

"What was her name?" I asked, desperate for any piece of her.

"Lyrik," the woman said, her face softening. "I don't know her second name, sorry, we are forbidden to use them once we come here. We are all Vasilica."

Something settled in me. A long-awaited answer to a question I never knew I needed.

Catalin, as she told me her name was, was the tenth wife in the current harem of twenty. She reminded me of Mama a bit. She had the same easy, warm way of talking.

Gheata was Prima Sotie, or first wife, the longest surviving wife of my sire, and the only woman of the Vasilican Drayvn to have survived the pregnancy and birth of not only one male heir, but two. Most likely because of her own Drayvn bloodline, as the daughter of a lower Drayvn lord, she had been saved from the usual fate of female offspring by being the first child born to the male.

"She is the mother of Domne Andrei and Domne Toma," Catalin explained in a hushed voice.

Which explained her apparent hatred of me. I had nearly killed her precious son.

I shivered, pulling a blanket around my shoulders as my breath misted in the air, getting up and crossing to the empty fireplace. There was a stack of wood next to it, all the implements to light it too, though they were covered in dust.

"Oh, no. No fire," Catalin whispered urgently, hurrying over to me as I reached for the wood.

"Why?" I asked, rubbing my cold hands together. "It's freezing in here."

Catalin huffed, pulling her blanket around her own shoulders. "Gheata's rules. She won't permit any of us to light a fire in here. She doesn't like the warmth.'

I blinked at her in confusion. "Why no—"

I was interrupted by the doors being flung open as Gheata

herself strode back in, scowling at Catalin who had shrunk back from me.

"I told *you* to stay in your chambers," she hissed.

Catalin fled back through the door she had emerged from without a backwards glance.

"Follow me," Gheata said coldly, her gown whispering against the stone floor as she turned and strode out.

I had to almost run to keep up with her as she led me through the eerie hallways of the castle. We passed a blur of Drayvn and Sylvyn faces, all of them looking at me with interest. I studied the faces one by one, looking for Andrei.

We paused at huge oak doors and Gheata swept to a halt, giving me a final once over before nodding her head to a stone-faced Sylvyn male.

The doors groaned as he pushed them open to reveal a surprisingly ornate room. It was richly decorated in plush rugs and tapestries. Paintings lined the walls of sceneries from seemingly all over the world. I stared at them as we passed, fascinated with the barren sand-covered landscape of one to the rich jungle of another, full of colour. It was so meticulously painted that it looked as if I could just step into the painting itself and breathe in the lush smells of the flowers.

"I see you are an admirer of art."

I turned to see my sire. Lord Vladimyre Visilica stood close enough that I could almost see my reflection in the dark obsidian of his eyes.

I straightened, clasping my hands behind my back as I surveyed him cooly. I would not let this monster see how he made my blood turn to ice whenever I felt his eyes on me.

"That will be all, Prima." My sire said quietly, not bothering to look at his wife as she curtseyed deeply to him and left without a word."

"They are a reminder to me of what exists in the world that I have not yet conquered," he said, turning to look at the jungle painting I had been so fascinated with.

"What do you want from me?" I asked. Fighting to keep my voice steady.

His attention turned back to me, and he reached to twirl a lock of my hair around his finger. "Have you bled yet?"

I pulled away from him, feeling my face heat the same way it had the last time I was asked that question. "No," I spat at him.

He nodded as if he had been expecting that. "There is time to find out what you are then. You are the only female Drayvn that I have ever found to have existed," he murmured. "You are valuable to me, daughter. I have produced some of the most powerful Drayvn in Mircian history, I have experimented with my bloodline, crossing them with Sylvyn of all races and I have seven heirs that will spread across the world and conquer it in my name."

The smile he gave me made the Drayvn in my blood stir, rising in answer to the threat of an apex predator.

"You were only meant to be a vassal for one of my higher lords. The heir you produce would be something not yet seen in Mircian history. A powerful, direct line of my blood." His claw ran along the underside of my chin. "But then you ripped the throat out of one of my strongest heirs," he breathed, his eyes fixed on mine. "You. A child, untrained and untested. Now I want to see what I have truly created before you are bred, what potential I can expect from your line."

The door clicked open behind us, and his attention went to whoever entered.

"You asked for me, My Lord?"

I turned to see Darius bowing to my sire.

"You are to begin her training," Vladimyre said, walking in a slow circle around me.

I saw Darius› eyes flare with surprise, but he masked it with a dip of his head.

"Of course," he murmured. "What training would you like her to receive?"

"All of it," Vladimyre said. "Push her. I want this—" his lip curled in disdain. "This *Sylvyn* side of her she clutches to destroyed. Make her into what she was born to be. I want to know if this mix of the race is something I can breed into a line, a mix that will improve on our genetics, or if is a weakness that needs to be eradicated."

CHAPTER NINE
Age Fifteen

I was screaming. Papa's neck torn under my fingers as I tried to hold the life inside him that was streaming hot over my fingers. Mama was calling my name, pleading with me to *run*. *Please run, Lyrik.*

I couldn't breathe, the screaming was in my ears, drowning everything except the rending pain in my heart as I looked into the cold eyes of Andrei. My brother. My enemy.

Hands were on my shoulders, and I lashed out at them, throwing them off me. Then his hand closed around my throat like it had been around Mama's, squeezing the life from me.

"*Lyrik,*" He snarled in my ear. Except it wasn't Andrei's voice. His voice would be burned in my mind forever. "*Such a pretty little flower,*" he had hissed in Mama's ear.

"Lyrik."

My mind cleared slightly, cold air cooling my body as I struggled past the horror wrapping itself through my mind.

"Wake up."

I came to myself with a jolt. My hands clutched at the one

pushing me into the bed, stopping me from attacking him.

Darius loomed over me. The doors to my small room flung open, women peering around them with wide eyes.

I could hear Gheata scolding them to get back to their rooms.

"You were dreaming," Darius said to me, his tone gentler than I had heard before as he released me slowly.

My throat hurt as if I had been screaming for hours. My head a low aching pulse.

"Get her under control," Gheata hissed from the doorway. "I have pregnant women in here that she is keeping up every damn night with her hysterics."

I had been here a month and the nightmares were not getting any better.

Gheata had been pushing for my removal from the harem from the day I was placed there, my sire placing me under her charge, to which she had venomously objected out of his hearing. After I had injured Natalia, one of the other wives as she had tried to wake me during a nightmare, Darius had been placed in rooms outside the entranceway down the hall to monitor me.

Darius hovered in the room, waiting for my mind to clear the remnants of the nightmare before leaving with a short nod back to his own rooms, and I was left in the coolness of mine, staring at the ceiling.

It would be daylight soon, and the misery of my new existence would continue. I ran my hands up my arms, feeling every cut and bruise on them. The marks of the 'training' I received every day, from sunup to sundown.

Darius was a fair teacher, though he pushed me harder than I thought necessary. But he was not there all the time, and the Drayvn that would take his place when he was called away were cruel.

Today was going to be particularly miserable. Today was my fifteenth birthday, and the only thing I wanted was Mama and Papa.

Maybe today would be the day I saw Andrei finally and would get the chance to kill him. He had been absent since my arrival, I heard from whispers within the harem that he had been rushed back to Corvin by Mihail, another of my brothers that I had not yet met, and healers had just been able to bring him back, though it had taken one of them to sacrifice for him, a healer's gift to give up their own life force to save another. I was guessing that was not by choice.

I found out that I had seven brothers, though my skin crawled at that word *brother*.

Kalias t, the eldest son, I had met. Andrei is the second, and son of Gheata. Mihail— third and Calib— fourth, I had not met yet. Emil— fifth son, shadows my sire everywhere he goes, his resemblance to Vladimyre was uncanny and at a glance, I got the two mixed. Sorin— the sixth son I had only seen at a distance but looked the same as the rest of them, with dark hair and pale skin and sharp features. Toma was the youngest son, though still somewhere in his thirties. Second son of Gheata and a sadistic, entitled Drayvn. Even his name makes the women of the harem quail.

I sighed, sitting up in bed and wincing at the cold air around me, pulling on my thick tunic before I pushed back the covers.

I padded into the stillness of the harem living area, nodding at one of the servants who rushed off, coming back moments later with a steaming pot of tea and a plate of food. I was only permitted to eat actual food at breakfast, the rest of my meals were blood. Not that I minded. My body was accustomed to feeding regularly, I had begun thirsting for it more, craving the satisfying fullness that I only seemed to get from blood and enjoying the additional strength it had given my body.

The Drayvn only feed. They seem to have a mingled fascination and disgust for my mixed diet.

"I thought I heard somebody up."

I blinked at Catalin, startled out of my growing anxiety as the start of my day›s training grew closer. "I couldn't sleep," I mumbled, knuckling my eyes. One side of my face was puffy still from yesterday›s training. My shoulder was stiff as well.

"I heard," Catalin said dryly. She shivered, pulling a throw around her shoulders as she nodded thanks to a servant that deposited her own breakfast in front of her. "The nightmares seem to be getting worse, rather than better."

I nodded grimly, pushing my food around my plate.

"Eat," Catalin said gently, her hand touching mine briefly. "You need to keep up your strength."

I flinched at the contact. I couldn't help it. The warmth of her skin on mine was so strange in this cold, unforgiving place.

The door creaked behind us, and we looked up to see Darius leaning in the doorway his brow quirked. "Since you are already up and seemingly uninterested in eating, we will start early," he said. "Dressed and downstairs in ten."

I shut my eyes and sighed, pushing my plate away from me.

Whack. The hit caught me off guard, a small noise escaping me as Darius' staff cracked across my middle.

"Legs straight," Darius barked as Drayvn across the far side of the training yard leered at me.

My arms were burning, the ropes around my wrists that had me suspended from a beam were cutting painfully into my skin and my stomach muscles were screaming their protest.

Crack. I saw the second hit coming as I struggled to lift my legs straight out in front of me again fast enough and bent a knee quickly, taking the hit painfully on my shin.

"Straighten your legs," Darius hissed again.

My legs were trembling with the effort at keeping them out

ahead. The muscles of my stomach and back past the point of cramping and moving into a steady, fiery burn that I knew would be agony as I tried to straighten again.

"You are weak, Lyrik," Darius said flatly, walking around me in a circle, the tip of his staff prodding me painfully in the ribs. "Shift, it will be easier for you if you let your Drayvn blood take dominance."

"No," I snarled, tasting blood from my lip that I had cruelly bitten.

Darius huffed a laugh, though there was no humour on his harsh face as he surveyed me. "Suit yourself."

I heard the hiss of a blade being drawn. A moment of fear slicing through me at my unprotected back before the ropes suspending me vibrated and I was falling. I hit the frozen ground hard, thoroughly winded and gasping for air as pain lanced up my spine.

A hand twisted into my hair, hauling me roughly to my feet before I could force air into my lungs as I was dragged, my hands grasping in vain against the ripping pull of my hair.

"Run," Darius said flatly, shoving me forward. "Around the outer ring of the yards until I tell you to stop."

I forced my quivering muscles to move, taking faltering steps forward until I managed to get a rhythm going, shaking my hands to get blood flow back into them. Last week Darius left me running for four hours. I had finally juddered to a halt and taken a beating from a Drayvn guard that had been left to watch over me for the disobedience.

I added the guard's face to the list of Drayvn I was going to kill.

My lungs burned as I kept a steady pace, keeping as far to the outside of the track as I could and away from the other Drayvn that littered the yard. Every single one of them just waiting for Darius to look away to get a shot in.

They despised me. Drayvn did not feel emotion in a normal

way. But they recognised a threat. I represented the unknown, the only female Drayvn known to have been born and none of them liked it. I could feel their eyes on me whenever I was out here in the open, like wolves watching a rabbit and it made my skin crawl.

I ran past pain, past exhaustion. My body fell into a distant hollowness as my legs moved on their own, in time to the rhythm of my breathing.

The shadows had moved a good metre across the ground, the only way I could measure time in these hours of agony when Darius stepped in front of my path again. He held a water skin and threw it at me, nearly knocking me on my ass as I fumbled to catch it and I drank deeply, wondering at the wiseness of it in case I had to continue running again. A belly full of water would be uncomfortable.

"Here." Darius was holding a staff the same as his out to me, and I eyed it cautiously. I hadn't been allowed to touch a weapon yet.

"Either you can take it, or I can beat you with it," Darius said, a smile curving his lips. "I don't mind which."

I handed the skin back, taking the staff quickly. It was smooth under my grasp, the wood heavier than I had anticipated, and slightly shorter than his.

"I probably shouldn't start you on this for another couple of months yet, but I am getting *rather* bored," he drawled, raking his long, dark hair back from his face and braiding it deftly before tucking the plait down his shirt.

"What do I do with it?" I asked. I was nervous, my hands sweating and making my grip precarious.

Darius moved further into the yard, planting his feet steadily and grinning at me. "Hit me."

I startled, looking down at my staff and then up at him. "What?"

"Hit me," he repeated. "I won't move my feet. Try and hit me."

I hesitated.

The blow hit me just above the ankle, taking my legs cleanly out beneath me and once again I found myself gasping on the ground, clutching my screaming limbs.

Darius peered down at me. "I don't enjoy repeating myself."

Groaning, I got to my feet, leaning on the staff.

He settled himself again, his staff held loosely, butt to the ground as he watched me. "Hit me," he said again.

Sending a prayer to the Gods, I swung, aiming for his head.

My staff cracked against his as he deflected the blow, the shockwave jarring up my arms and making me drop the staff. A second later, pain exploded up my ribs and I doubled over, crying out at the agony.

"Lesson one," Darius said calmly. "Never drop your weapon. Pick it up."

Every breath in hurt and I desperately fought the tears that were burning against my eyelids, but I bent over and retrieved my staff.

Darius rested his staff against the ground again. Surveying me cooly. "Hit me."

I swung again, this time when my staff clunked into his I was expecting it, bracing against the jarring. I drew it back ready to hit again before pain exploded again across my ribs in the same spot, taking my breath away. I screamed, my knees crashing into the ground, my staff clattering next to me as I curled around the ripping agony in my side.

"Lesson two," Darius said, "do not give your enemy such a huge opening. You left your entire flank exposed with that swing, keep your arms down. Short, sharp hits in this close to one another. Pick it up."

Something was moving in my side as I breathed. Agonising pain with every breath. My hand closed around my staff, and I used it to push myself to my feet, trying, and failing to stand straight against the rending fire that tugged in my side.

"Hit me."

I swung and missed. I heard the crack of bone this time as his staff took me again in the same spot. My vision erupted into bright lights and then went black.

CHAPTER TEN

"No, no. Don't sit up just yet." Hands were on my arms as I scrabbled to get up. My fingers clawed at the dirt beneath me. Except it wasn't dirt. Sheets were tangled around me and my face rested against a pillow. I tried to open my eyes and couldn't. Panic filled me. I was blind.

"Easy, Lyrik."

It was Natalia's soft, soothing voice that filtered through my senses.

"The healer is working on you now; your ribs are healed, but your face is swollen badly. Just wait a moment."

Her words registered as I felt cool hands moving over my face, the tightness of it gradually receding until the light began to filter back to me. My eyes slowly began to open, realising they had been swollen shut and I blinked at the afternoon sun, tears streaming out of my watering eyes. I was in my room again. Natalia sat next to my bed; her face tight as she watched the woman work.

The healer had been here many times. She was on an older servant, her hands withered and bony and her healing gift small, but she had taken care of me many times over when my muscles had torn from exertion, or a Drayvn had got in a blow out of Darius view.

"Did you and Darius fight?" Natalia asked, her eyes wide as she ran them down my body.

I groaned. "I wouldn't call it that."

The healer waved for me to roll on my side, running her hands a final time over the side that Darius had targeted. It didn't hurt to breathe now, but they were still tender.

"I haven't got enough left in me to take the deeper bruising away," she said, her voice thin and wavering. "Once I am replenished tomorrow, I can come back and finish that."

"I'm sure there will be more for you tomorrow anyway," I muttered, nodding my thanks and sitting up gingerly. I felt like I had been trampled by a stampede of horses and my belly ached with hunger. I felt hollow and sore.

"Your... supper, was brought up not long ago," Natalia said, taking my elbow as a wave of dizziness overcame me. She led me down the hall into the living area, my bare feet freezing against the stone floor, and I went straight to the goblet of rich blood waiting for me on the massive dining table.

I cringed at the half-cold metallic taste of it. I could barely stomach it cold and put it back down in disgust. I shivered, tucking my aching arms against my body as I stared at the barren fireplace.

Last birthday I had sat with Mama in front of the roaring fire, listening to one of Papa's stories, warm and happy. Papa had slaughtered a sheep for me, letting me feed until I was drowsy and content.

Now they were gone. There were no stories. No love. No fire and I was hurting, from my broken heart to the tips of my fingers.

Catalin slipped into the seat next to me, wrapped up against the chill of the air and uncurled her arm, tying to pull me into the warmth of her cocoon. Her scent filled my senses, calming my frayed nerves, a small warmth in this pit of torment.

Cold. Everything here was cold. My eyes fell on the stack of firewood next to the giant hearth and something snapped in me.

I stalked to the fireplace, groaning as I lowered myself in front of it and began to stack wood and kindling in its huge mouth.

"Lyrik, what are you doing?" Natalia hissed, hurrying over to hover behind me. She kept throwing nervous glances at the doorway that led to the adjoining rooms.

"I'm cold," I snapped, anger coursing through me.

"You can't!" Catalin said, sounding half panicked. Gheata forbids it!"

"Gheata can kiss my ass," I muttered, sliding one of the long matches from the mouth of the carved Druka of the fireplace, and lighting it with a flick of my wrist against a piece of wood. I watched in satisfaction as the dry log took instantly, roaring to life in the fireplace.

The heat hit my skin, prickling along my face and up my frozen arms. I glanced up at Catalin and Natalia, both women entranced as they watched the flames licking their way along the wood.

Clambering to my feet again, I picked up the small teapot that stood against the edge of the fireplace, and retrieved my abandoned supper, pouring it into it and hanging it on the curved hook over the flames. The heat from the fire had nearly warmed me to my core by the time I took the teapot off again, pouring the now warm blood back into my mug and taking long, satisfied draws of it.

I felt the strength flooding into my arms again, my legs. Heat curled in my belly, melding with the heat from the flames. It was the first time in months I had been truly warm.

"What is this?"

Natalia and Catalin jumped up from where they had sunk down next to me, shrinking back as Gheata stormed over to us, her face black with rage. "Who lit that."

I closed my eyes for a moment, the golden light of the fire

shining through them before draining the last of my mug in one swallow and standing to face her.

"I did."

"Put it out," Gheata hissed, her eyes black with anger. "Immediately."

She was taller than me, I barely came up to her chest and it irritated me to have to look up at her. Something surged in me, a wash of anger and defiance that was new, yet I welcomed it wholeheartedly.

"No."

Gheata's eyes flared, her mouth thinning into a line and her eyes narrowing in a way that marred the attractiveness of her beautiful face. She shifted, her arms lifting in a way that I knew she was about to slap me.

A calmness settled over me, my body loosening and settling as it slipped into a languid, predatory stance. I felt the rumble deep in my chest, felt the prick of my fangs as they descended, my lips drawing back as I snarled at her. I let every piece of the bitterness I was holding onto melt into the sound, let my Drayvn blood rise.

Gheata froze, her hand still pulled back to strike as her face paled.

"Strike me, and I will rip that arm from your body," I hissed.

She stared at me a moment, her arm slowly lowering until she held it awkwardly beside her again, her eyes flashing with anger.

"I am cold," I said, my voice as icy as any Drayvn. I flung my arm out towards Catalin and Natalia. "They are *all* cold. This fire is going to be lit day and night from now on, and if you have an issue with that *Prima*. You can fight me for it and see where that leaves you."

Catalin and Natalia were staring at me, their eyes as wide as saucers.

Gheata's eyes narrowed, but she said nothing, turning and stalking away in a billow of skirts.

I caught movement in the entranceway across the room, my attention snapping to it. Darius stood, leaning against the doorframe. One brow was quirked, a smirk on his lips. He caught my gaze, holding it for a moment, before giving me a small nod and slipping out of the doorway and disappearing.

I didn't see Gheata for the rest of the night, though the living quarters quickly filled with women as the air around us warmed with the huge fireplace.

Catalin sent servants to bring up more wood and I began to feel self-conscious as the women nervously approached me, some brushing their fingers against me in thanks, some ducking their heads, or offering me small tokens of appreciation.

I just wanted to be left alone, curled up on the pillow I had pilfered from the pile in the corner, my toes stretched out to the flames.

"They are grateful," Catalin murmured to me as she lowered herself onto her own pillow at my side, sighing in happiness as she held her hands to the flames and leaned her shoulder against mine in easy companionship. "No one has stood up to Gheata in many, many years."

I frowned at the flames, sipping on the tea one of the women had poured for me.

"Not since your mother."

I almost choked. My heart constricting in my chest.

"You are a lot like her," Catalin said softly. "Gheata hated her, Lyrik would have her almost spitting flames."

I turned to study her. She had a small smile on her lips as she watched the flames. "She would sing some nights, right here in front of the fire. Sometimes we would join in. For those moments, I could almost forget where I was." Her green eyes glanced around the room. "Almost."

"How long have you been here?" I asked.

She paused for a moment, a small frown crossing her brow as she contemplated. "Thirty-two years," she said eventually. "Thirty-two years, and three daughters lost to me." She threw me a haunted smile. "Maybe I will be blessed with a son next, and I will be free of this place. To roam the forest with my girls."

I didn't know what to say. There *was* nothing to say and I realised at that moment, it was not just me here in my grief.

"At least we have a fire again," she offered as if sensing my loss of words. Her nose crinkled as she gave me a grin that lit her entire face up. "I'm never going to forget her face when you threatened her."

Natalia dropped to my other side, chuckling darkly. "Neither will I," she said. She held up her mug to me, clinking it against mine. "None of us will forget it."

Chapter Eleven

"You are dropping your arm," Darius warned, seconds before I deflected the blow he aimed at my head.

"I'm not!" I protested.

His staff cracked down onto my shoulder, and I winced.

"You would have deflected that if you weren't dropping your fucking arm," he said cooly.

I swore, rolling my head and flexing my shoulder. I had been training with the staff for three months. I was picking it up fast, though I made sure to keep my movements slow and clunky at times, especially after long training sessions, letting Darius believe I was worse than I was.

"Get up on your toes, you are still walking like a brick on legs," he sighed.

I glared at him, blocking the upward swing of his staff and stepping out of the range of the next.

"Good," he said, swiping away my counter strike with the flat of his hand. "That was sloppy though."

I muttered profanities under my breath, scowling at him as he wandered over to take a drink. I was sweating profusely; I could feel it running in rivulets down my back. He wasn't even flushed, the prick.

He grinned at me, holding out the water and I shook my head, holding my staff in the air and twisting to stretch my back out while I waited for him.

Darius straightened as two Drayvn approached us, both surveying me coldly. Toma and a stranger.

"Domne Mihail, Domne Toma," Darius greeted them, ducking his head in a bow.

I surveyed Mihail, the older of the two. He did not look like the rest of my brothers, his skin was slightly more olive-toned compares to the paleness of the rest of them, his hair slightly auburn in the sunlight.

"Sister," Mihail said, cocking his head as he looked me up and down.

Toma's lip curled at the address, his white fangs glinting in the sun. "I wouldn't go that far," he murmured.

"I'm willing to agree with you on that count," I replied sarcastically, giving Toma a mocking curtsey.

His eyes narrowed on me a moment, before glancing over my shoulder. "Lord Vasilica wants a report of her progress."

"I have been reporting to him directly, but... she is progressing slowly," Darius replied, leaning against his staff. "Emphasis on the slow."

I bristled, glaring at him over my shoulder.

"She's still in lower form, that's why," Toma said, looking disgusted. "Why haven't you gotten her to shift yet."

"I'm standing right here you know," I snapped.

Toma slid his eyes to me, stepping towards me until he was close enough to feel his cool breath on my face. "Answer me then. You are Drayvn, are you not? That is the sole extent of your worth, why our sire is using you in this little experiment of his, yet you cover it in this lower form that is *weak.*" He stepped back, circling me slowly. "Why Father wanted to see you trained is beyond me. You are never going to amount to more than your worth in the hareem."

I bared my teeth at him, and Mihail huffed a laugh.

"Brother," he warned. "You are here to observe."

"Andrei did not find me weak," I hissed at Toma. I hadn't meant to say it, my temper speaking for me, and I saw Toma's face darken as he snarled at me.

I braced for the strike, feeling my body loosen and drop into a crouch, ready for the attack as a large hand curled around the back of my neck, yanking me backwards.

Darius shook me until I saw stars, his hand gripping my neck hard enough to make it pop.

"You will address your brothers with respect," he said, his voice low.

My knees jarred against the cold ground as he pushed me to the floor, still gripping me painfully as he made me look up at the two Drayvn.

Mihail had a restraining hand on Toma, whose face was dark with anger.

"Shift, Sister," Mihail ordered, his face impassive.

"No," I bit out, wincing as Darius squeezed harder.

"Why do you fight it?" Mihail asked, curiously. "Would it not be easier to let your Drayvn blood make this training easier? Feel less pain, not struggle so."

I didn't answer, my gaze on the dirt in front of me.

Mihail's boots edged into my vision, a cold, sharp claw rasping under my chin and lifting my face to him.

"You *will* break," he warned. "Father wants to see what you are capable of. That is not achieved in lower form. Either you will shift, or we will force it."

I just stared at him, my reflection looking back at me from those emotionless, black eyes."

"Suit yourself," Mihail murmured. "Do not say I didn't warn you." He stood up, waving a hand to Darius to release me.

I felt him hesitate a moment, then coolness surrounded my neck as his hand lifted away, only to be replaced by Mihail's clawed hand as he hauled me across the yard to the two posts that were sunk into the frozen ground.

It only took moments for him to have me tied between them, my arms stretched between the two posts.

My stomach lurched at the cruel smile Toma had on his face and I fought to keep my face blank as he paced slowly in front of me.

Darius was standing stiffly to one side, his hands clasped behind his back and a small frown on his face. "Domne Mihail, if you give me longer in my process, I believe I will get the results Lord Vasilica requires," he began, but Mihail cut him off with a raised hand.

Mihail came to stand in front of me, leaning down to look into my face. "Last chance, Sister. Shift, or I will force you to."

I spat in his face. Only the satisfaction of seeing his disgust held the rising terror in me at bay as he straightened and wiped his cuff across his cheek.

He disappeared behind me, and I heard the rending tear of my shirt, and then ice-cold air caressed the skin of my back. My shirt billowed in the breeze, trapping the cold air around me as it was caught in the torn fabric.

I heard the crack and felt the impact before the pain registered, and then seconds later the white-hot fire of it ripped through my body. It felt like a line of molten metal had been poured across my back. I couldn't scream, I couldn't even breathe for a moment, just took gulping mouthfuls of air into lungs that seemed intent on staying empty.

Mihail appeared in front of me again, a dark-handled whip in his hands, the end of it trailing on the ice-covered ground.

I could almost breathe again, air rasping into my lungs as the stars in my vision receded. Only for the fire across my back to flare hotter by the second.

"Shift, Sister."

I could hear Mama's voice echo in my mind. *Lyrik, don't lose yourself*

I clamped my teeth together and forced down the surge that had risen in me.

Mihail shrugged and disappeared again.

I didn't even have time to brace myself before the next crack came. I screamed this time as fire exploded across my back in a scorching stripe.

Mihail was in front of me again. "Shift, Sister."

"Go fuck a pig," I hissed at him.

Crack.

The next stripe made my ears ring, blackness lurking in the corner of my vision and a sob escaped my lips.

"Mihail." I faintly heard Darius› voice. It sounded edged with anger and Toma's snapped reply silenced him.

Crack.

"Shift, Sister."

Crack.

Blackness overcame me, and I ran towards it willingly.

I was lying in my bed. I had swum towards consciousness a while before, but I did not have the energy to grasp it fully. My back was a dull ache that spiked with pain upon every breath.

I could hear voices murmuring outside. The crackle and pop of the huge fireplace and the muffled sound of boots on stone as someone walked past my room. Turning my head slowly I opened my eyes, letting the room slowly come into view, and froze.

Darius was sitting in a large armchair next to my bed, one foot propped on the edge, his eyes closed and his head leaning back against the wall. I watched him a moment, taking the opportunity to scrutinize him closely. In sleep the hard lines of his face relaxed slightly, softening the harshness of his features. His severe brow and slightly long, aristocratic nose could almost have been unnatractive… yet somehow it all came together into a strangely handsome yet brutish mix. His skin was sun bronzed— a vast difference from the paleness of the Drayvn, and while he had the usual Sylvyn skin— unmarred from the ravages of time until they reached into centuries of existance, he had small scars from what must have been years of intense training. There was a fine line of a faded scar running from the corner of his eye that gave the impression of laugh lines. I almost huffed in amusement at the thought of him ever laughing enough to get them, even if he did live as long as some of the elderly Sylvyn I had met.

His hair was braided back in his usual style, the sides slightly bristled from a few days growth. I don't know why but seeing that, the slightly unkempt look made him feel slightly more… normal.

I moved my arm up beneath myself, trying to shift into a better position. The movement flexed the muscles of my abused back, a whimper slipping from my lips.

Darius› eyes snapped open, his foot falling off the bed as he sat up with a start, blinking rapidly as if trying to gather himself before his gaze fell on me.

"I have called a healer, but they are the town over and will not be here until tomorrow with the storm coming in," he said matter of factly. "You need to eat; you have been out since yesterday."

"I'm not hungry," I muttered.

"I don't care. You eat, or you don't heal. You don't heal, then training is going to be miserable for you," he stated. He whistled loudly and a servant appeared moments later, bobbing respectfully as Darius ordered supper to be brought in for me.

We waited in silence until it arrived. The rich scent of blood filled the room.

My stomach heaved at the smell, nausea washing over me.

"Your stomach is empty, and your body is pushed past its limit trying to heal," Darius said, noticing my expression. "You will feel better after you feed."

He held the cup to my lips, awkward as the angle was, and helped me take small sips from it.

I felt the effects immediately. Strength returned to my limbs and the tingling in my back that suggested the advanced healing of the Drayvn was already beginning to close the wounds Mihail had inflicted on me.

He didn't talk as he fed me, pressing the cup to my lips as soon as he had seen me swallow until it was empty, though his face had a tenseness to it I had not seen before.

"I wouldn't do that," he warned as I moved to push myself upright.

I hissed as I felt skin tug and move.

"It's open to the bone in two places," he said quietly.

"I'm going to kill him," I hissed, then froze. I hadn't meant to say it. I glanced at him, but he just surveyed me with a raised brow.

"Why didn't you shift?" He asked.

I didn't answer him, wishing I could close my eyes and slip back into the darkness.

"You could have avoided all of that," he pushed.

I huffed. "You think if I had shown them what they wanted, they wouldn't have baited me into attacking them?" I asked coldly. "They do not want me here. I am a threat to everything they have been raised to believe."

"And what is that?" Darius asked quietly.

I turned my head slowly, meeting his gaze and holding it. "That I am a female, and capable of ripping them apart. They can beat me. They can hurt me as I am now, but I am not a true threat to them until I shift. My sire knows what I am, he has seen it himself, they haven't. If you think that stunt today was on his orders, then you are an idiot. They cannot kill me as I am now, because my sire would punish them. They could kill me in self-defence though."

Darius› brows rose and he sat back in his chair, a finger to his lips as he pondered my words. He laughed softly, shaking his head. "Wise beyond your years. You may just survive them yet."

CHAPTER TWELVE

I woke to Gheata's cold voice outside my room. The healer had come last night, four days late, held off by the bitter storm that had lashed the country mercilessly.

I pushed myself upright as she entered my rooms, her face pulled into the usual grimace of distaste she usually had while looking at me.

"You have not given your clothes to the laundry for a week. Where are you hiding them?"

I blinked at her. "What?"

"Your clothes," she snapped, "Where are you hiding them?"

I glanced at my usual servant who was quailing in the doorway behind her, arms full of the towels and sheets that had been stripped from my bed last night after my wounds had been closed. They had scarred, after being left to heal naturally for so long, and I had stared at them in the mirror. A reminder to myself as to what this place was.

I plucked at the loose shift I was wearing. "You can have this if you want it?" I raised a brow at her... "Or I can find you my dirty training clothes from last week." I pointed to a basket in the corner. "I think they went it there."

She glared at me, crossing to the basket and pulling out the shredded clothes. I stared at them a moment. The white shirt I had been wearing was nearly completely brown from dried blood, stiff and shredded in her hands. She threw it aside and picked up my trousers and undergarments which were only marginally better.

I felt my face heat as she held them up, inspecting them.

"What are you doing?" I hissed.

She seemed to satisfy herself with the clothing and threw it back in the basket, wiping her hands on one of the towels the servants grappled with.

"Where are the rest of them?" She asked.

"I have no others," I bit out. "I haven't moved off this damn bed all week. Are you going to tell me why you are going through my undergarments like a creep?"

Her lip twitched in the faintest of smiles. It turned my stomach and made the hairs rise on my arms to see it.

"His lordship has asked that I inform him when you have your first blood," she said cooly. "The servants reported you were hiding your items, and it is my duty to find the truth."

My face flamed. "You are disgusting," I spat at her. "Get out."

Gheata shrugged slightly, sweeping out of the room without a second glance at me.

My mortification was made worse when I saw Darius leaning against the doorframe, and from the look on his face, he had heard everything. He bowed his head at Gheata respectfully as she passed, waiting until her footsteps had disappeared before he straightened again.

"I see you are feeling better," he said cooly as if the last few minutes had not happened.

I nodded jerkily, not trusting my voice.

"Good. We start after breakfast. I will meet you back here in thirty minutes." He disappeared as silently as he had arrived, leaving me blinking at the doorway, trying to process everything that had just happened.

Mama had explained how woman's bodies worked. I knew exactly what she was looking for and what the implication meant. It was a looming clock above my head. I would not contemplate escape until I had my revenge, and Andrei had not shown himself since my arrival.

I dressed quickly and padded into the harem living quarters, most of the women were already up and eating at the huge dining table. I slipped into a seat next to Natalia, murmuring my good mornings to them.

Another of the wives, Emalia was down a few seats, looking sallow and exhausted. She was six months pregnant, and I had heard it was a suspected male, because of how hard the pregnancy had been, and Gheata was busy fussing over her. The only time I saw Gheata show any kind of warmth to these women was when they carried a child within them.

"I'm glad to see you on your feet," Natalia murmured, pushing a plate of fruit towards me.

I nodded, absently cutting a pear into slices and biting into the sweet fruit.

"Are you returning to the training already?" Catalin asked, her brow furrowing in alarm.

I nodded again, clearing my throat. "The healer did their job."

Catalin shook her head, turning back to her food.

I didn't strike up conversation with them as I finished my food and sat quietly, sipping the fragrant hot tea that was always on hand here. It was getting harder to want to talk to anyone, I felt distanced from these women as if, even though my Drayvn blood was shoved down as deep as I could get it, it still whispered in my ear.

A name I was always half listening for grabbed my attention and my focus snapped to Gheata, sitting between a few of the women and eating her breakfast. She had a self-satisfied air to her, a look of smug pride on her face.

"Domne Andrei left for Attica this morning, they are meeting with the new queen there to discuss the druka taming that she has mastered.

My stomach fell. He was gone. Attica was months of travel there and back, months that I would be here, waiting for my chance to avenge Mama and Papa.

I noticed Darius return and slipped out of my chair, approaching him on silent feet, my body heavier than it had been moments before.

"You have eaten enough?" He asked, my cloak and a heavy tunic over his arm.

I nodded.

"Put this on," he said, handing me the clothing. "You are going to need it."

"Where are we going?" I asked. There was snow in the air, a good layer of it underfoot that crunched as we walked towards the two horses that were waiting in the courtyard.

"To train," Darius said as if I were an idiot.

"Not here?" I asked.

"You gonna keep asking dumb questions, or can we get moving?" Darius said, giving me an exasperated look.

I glowered at him as he mounted his horse in a fluid movement before I stared helplessly up at my horse. It was far taller than our mules had been. The stirrup dangling by my chin. I reached for it, trying to contemplate the best way to clamber up.

One of the sylvyn grooms cleared his throat and bent, his hands clasped in a cradle.

Darius snorted.

I ignored him, feeling my cheeks heat. "Thank you," I murmured to the groom as I placed my foot in his hands and he hoisted me onto the mare. I refused to look at Darius as the groom quickly shortened the stirrups for me, lifting my leg for the man to get to the buckles.

"Ready?" Darius asked mockingly.

I nodded, nudging my horse to follow him out the gates.

We rode out, our horses walking shoulder to shoulder, their hooves muffled on the snow. The forest ahead of us was gloomy and barren. I heard a wolf howling off in the distance and couldn't help the shiver that ran through me at the mournful sound, so beautiful and fierce at the same time.

"I would advise you not to contemplate running," Darius said casually, giving me a lopsided smile. He patted the crossbow that hung from a strap at his knee. "I would rather not have to shoot you, if I can help it."

I scowled at him from under my hood. "Why are we not training in the castle grounds?"

"Do you *want* to get whipped within an inch of your life again?" He pulled his cloak around him tighter, his breath misting the air in front of him as he spoke. "Your sire did not order them to do that. I inquired."

I kept my eyes on my horse›s ears. "I told you that."

He grunted and I felt his eyes on me as we rode, the silence stretching uncomfortably.

"How did you come to be in their employ?" I asked, genuinely curious. The castle was teeming with life, though very few of the residents with the level of respect Darius had, were Sylvyn.

"My great grandsire owned the castle," Darius said simply. "Our family ruled this district centuries ago. When the Drayvn rose, my grandsire convinced his father to swear allegiance to the Vasilica bloodline, threw all his eggs into one basket, so to speak. In return, the grounds were purchased from us, rather than the alternative, and our family were insured a place within its court." He eyed me a moment. "My father was Secundar to the lord until he was killed in battle trying to take the northern keep for your sire."

I frowned. "Secundar?"

"His right hand. Advisor." He stretched in the saddle, "Your sire is one of the most ruthless rulers this kingdom has ever seen, do you know how he has kept his dominance over this land for longer than any other in history?"

I shook my head.

"He knows his limitations." He was silent a moment as we veered off onto a narrower path, my horse having to fall into step behind his as we picked our way around some boulders. I drew up beside him again as the path opened back out again.

"What limitations does a Drayvn have?" I asked. I tried not to look as interested as I was. Limitations meant weakness.

"Their inability to understand emotion," Darius replied, glancing at me. "Thinking as they do, sometimes they cannot comprehend the actions of the Sylvyn, cannot understand how a man would risk everything to save his wife, or why an enemy force would not surrender when they are the only thing standing between them and their children. That is why he is so invested in what you are."

I mulled his words over for a moment. "What has that got to do with me?"

"Because a Drayvn that could understand this, while being able to harness the strength of the Drayvn, the ruthlessness at will." He shook his head. "Your sire is well aware of the value of that, and so are your brothers."

"Except to my brothers, I am the threat that could replace them," I said quietly.

Darius huffed softly. "No. You are the one that could *provide* the threat. Don't forget that. At the end of the day, your sire views you as an interesting experiment, but you are still just livestock to him."

I pulled my horse up. "Why are you telling me this?" ·

I waited for him to bring his horse back around, until we were almost knee to knee, surveying each other. Close enough to see the thinly masked anger that lay behind his cool expression.

"Because *Vladimyre* has deemed it fit to put me on babysitting duty. I have served as Secundar to him for your lifetime twice over, and if I let you get killed by your brothers, it is all in vain. I have not worked this hard, done unimaginable things to get to this point, to lose my position *or* my life because of you."

I didn't miss his lapse in composure. The disdain he let slip as he said my sire›s name. It was a slight that could have gotten him killed in the castle had anyone overheard, and I tucked it away for later. I straightened in the saddle, lifting my chin to his glare.

"And how do you propose to keep my brothers from killing me."

He smiled then, and it didn't meet his eyes. It sent a shiver through me.

"I only have to keep you alive until your blood arrives, then you are no longer my problem. If we train out here, it will provide you with a level of protection"

It suited me. I had months until Andrei would return. Months to hone my body into something that could take the life from him the same way he had taken from Mama and Papa. All I had to do was survive until then.

Chapter Thirteen

Six months later

"Are you still fucking sleeping?"

Something thudded into my chest, and I jolted awake, a rumbling snarl ripping from my chest.

Darius was leaning against my doorway smirking, my other boot in his hands ready to lob that too.

"Piss off, Darius, you said I could have today off."

"I *said* you could have a sleep-in," he amended. "Or more, *I* could have a sleep in, and you got one by association."

I groaned, putting my pillow over my head and ignoring him.

A rough hand closed over my ankle, and I yelped, grabbing the sheets in vain as I was yanked rudely out of the bed and deposited on the floor.

"Get up, get dressed," he said. "You missed breakfast, I will have something sent up for you."

"*Fuuuuuuuuucckk,*" I breathed, flopping back on the floor and pushing the heel of my palms into my eyes. "It's been six months, Darius, can I not just have one day off?"

"Negative," Darius quipped, tossing my boot over his shoulder as he strode back to my door. "You don't get a day off, until your right hook doesn't suck worse than a geriatric quadriplegic."

I grunted as the boot landed squarely on my stomach and I threw it back at him, missing his head by centimetres as it thunked into the doorframe.

"See," he called back, disappearing out the doorway. "Useless."

I pulled the finger at his disappearing back, muttering to myself ways I was going to attempt to kick his ass today as I pulled on the supple, fur-lined clothes I had taken to wearing. I had lost the slightly rounded curves I had had when I came here, lean muscle replacing every inch of my body instead. It had made me feel the cold much more than I had before however, and Darius enjoyed taunting me for the layers of clothing I would pile on.

He reappeared as I was lacing my boots and shoved a breakfast cake into one of my hands.

"Can I not sit for breakfast?" I protested as he gave me a shove towards the door.

"Sure, as long as it's on your horse." He threw a water skin at me which I only just caught, nearly dropping my breakfast in the process.

"I hate you," I muttered.

"It's mutual," Darius grinned, winking at me. "Ready?"

"What is the rush?"

"We have company today," was his only reply.

My heart skipped and my steps faltered, I had to jog a few paces to catch back up with him. "Who?" I asked, dread filling me.

I had barely seen my brothers since my training had changed locations. Darius and I would leave immediately after breakfast and not return until late when I would fall into bed after supper.

No male was permitted into the harem living quarters except Darius, not that they had any desire to do so. Touching one of Lord Vasilica's wives was a death sentence, even for his sons, so I had not seen anyone other than the women in months.

I saw Darius exhale a long breath, misting in the cold air around him. He looked slightly on edge, and it made me nervous.

"Your sire," he said quietly as we reached the courtyard.

Lord Vasilica was already waiting for us, mounted on his horse alongside ours. He didn't so much as acknowledge me as I approached.

One of the grooms gave me a leg up onto my mare, tossing me my reigns and giving me a wink. He was a nice man, he always boosted me up to my saddle without me needing to ask, as if he saw how irritated it made me to ask for help and didn't fuss over me as some of the others did, checking my stirrups as if I were a child out for a morning ride.

"My Lord." Darius bowed to Lord Vasilica before mounting his gelding.

I glanced sideways at my sire, trying to gauge if my lack of deference had irritated him, but his face had the usual bland indifference of the Drayvn.

We rode out, me trailing the two of them.

Darius didn't even glance around to check that I was following, and it bit at me slightly, how easy he was in assuming I would follow like a meek pup.

He still had that crossbow hanging by his knee, I still had hatred in my heart. I knew which one was keeping me here, and it wasn't the risk of an arrow in my back.

I caught bits of their conversation as we rode and my anger rose, a bitter taste in my mouth as I heard my name multiple times. Talking about me as if I were not even here.

Darius was running over our normal training regime, which weapons he had permitted me to use... which wasn't many, and what we would be working on next.

I had to bite my lip to stop myself from blurting out something that would no doubt land me running laps until darkest night. The last time that had happened had been three weeks ago. I had called Darius a dog fucking whoreson when he had broken one of my fingers. I still had blisters on my feet.

I dismounted, feeling the most unsure of myself I had in months. I could feel Vladimyre watching my every movement as I approached the two of them, slowly wrapping my knuckles with a strip of fabric.

"Daughter." My sire finally greeted me.

"Vladimyre," I said back cooly. I saw Darius shift slightly on his feet. The only sign of his disapproval, and a warning.

Vladimyre's eyes narrowed at the blatant disregard of his status, but he smiled slightly, a curve of his lips that bared the tip of a fang.

"Darius tells me you are progressing well, and Prima Gheata informs me you are still not a woman."

I raised my brows at Darius. "Huh," I huffed. "That's funny, Darius tells me I'm a useless waste of Drayvn blood."

Darius wasn't fast enough to mask the flash of surprise across his face as his eyes flicked to mine in... was that amusement?

"I will see for myself," Vladimyre said, clearly missing the joke. He circled me once, and I fought to keep myself still during the inspection especially when I felt his cold, clawed finger push my thick plait aside and trace the line of the whip scar that ran up the back of my neck.

"You did not shift during this."

It wasn't a question, the lack of emotion in the statement as he surveyed the damage his son had inflicted made me nauseous.

He came around me to face me again, cocking his head to the side in a way that reminded me of a wolf. "You will not shift to save your own skin, nor during the training that pushes even my Drayvn soldiers, yet you shift for Mrs. Damaris."

Mama's name on his tongue made me want to scream, rage filtering through the tight leash I had on it and rising to a low growl in my throat. Something about this man drove me faster towards losing control than anything had before.

He smiled again, just the barest tilt to his lips. "Interesting."

He stepped back and waved a hand to Darius to start, watching intently as we moved into our normal training pattern.

Darius started us with staff, the weapon I was most used to.

I could hold my own with it, barely. My ribs thanked me for it. The first thing I had learned after that day when he had cracked and displaced three of my ribs was to shield from his blows, and I could occasionally get in a return blow now, which he always deflected with ease.

He must have been distracted today, however. Vladimyre watching must have irked him more than his cool exterior let on, because we were only in our fourth set when I saw the briefest of openings, and with a short lunge managed to land a sharp jab to his shoulder.

We paused and reset, though I could see it had rattled him. I gave him a grin, playing on his irritation.

He narrowed his eyes at me and the next set he took my legs out cleanly, winding me thoroughly as I hit the hard ground.

I was still grinning though as he waited for me to get up.

"What?" He snapped under his breath as we locked in close to each other in a stalemate.

"I got you," I hissed, my arms straining under the pressure he was putting on me. "Did that hurt?" I took advantage of the momentary rage that rippled across his face, as off guard as he was leaning down to hiss at me and head-butted him. Squarely in the nose.

The impact made me see stars, pain lancing through my head, but the muffled crack and the grunt of pain that came from him was worth it.

I lost the next three sets badly, taking heavy hits from his staff that I could feel welting under my clothes until I saw him make the same opening as before, and I managed to land another jab to his shoulder.

"Enough."

We both froze at the command from Vladimyre. He was eyeing me with interest as he stalked towards us. He narrowed his eyes at Darius.

"You are going easy on her."

Darius stiffened. "I am giving her the same training as I have given every one of your sons."

Vladimyre nodded that predatory look in his eye again. "But she is not one of my sons, is she?" He turned to me again, his expression contemplative. "You are finding his weaknesses? My sons could not land a blow on Darius so early."

I could almost see Darius bristling as I frowned in confusion.

"She is riling you," Vladimyre stated, still watching me. "Are you are doing it on purpose? Using his anger to weaken him, and then taking advantage of it?"

He reached a hand for Darius› staff. "What happens when your opponent does not take that bait, I wonder."

I barely had the chance to lift my staff to block him, the reverberations as his staff met mine jarring down both arms.

His attack was relentless, blow upon blow coming at me from every angle. I didn't catch them all, taking a hard blow to my side, my arm, and another to my thigh. I snarled at him as a move had his side pressing up against me, his taller body bearing down against my block. His face was impassive, not one ounce of effort on his face, and I knew at that moment he was barely trying at all.

It made me irrationally angry, and I dropped the staff, taking the painful blow to my shoulder, his side turned to me long enough to swing my fist, feeling satisfaction as it connected with his chest.

His blow connected with my jaw a second later, sending me sprawling, bright lights flickering in the corner of my vision.

I was on my feet in an instant, spitting my blood onto the ground and dropping into the fighting stance that Darius had drilled into me so thoroughly these months. He had made me stay in this position until I had cried at the muscles cramping up my legs and back. Not now though. Now my blood was singing, and it was taking everything in me to keep it down, to stop it from rising to the threat before me.

Vladimyre drew his lips back over his fangs, hissing at me.

It distracted me long enough to miss the tells of his strike, his hand wrapping around my throat as his teeth sunk into the arm I threw up in defence.

I slashed his face with my free hand, not realising my claws had lengthened until I saw the bright red lines well across his forehead.

Then I was flying, hitting a tree behind me with enough force that I heard something crack, praying it was wood and not bone as I crumpled to the floor, pain blossoming up my spine.

I peered up at him as he moved towards me, watching with satisfaction as one of my claw marks welled, a drip of blood sliding slowly down his forehead, tracing the side of his sharp nose.

"You were doing well until your anger got in the way," he mused softly. "It's a double-edged sword I see." He turned to Darius who was strolling up to his side. "Push her harder. She's capable of more."

"Of course." Darius bowed his head as Vladimyre left without a backwards glance.

Chapter Fourteen

"You're back early," Natalia said as I traipsed back into the harem, feeling like every muscle in my body was screaming in pain. I nodded, holding my fingers over my split lip to staunch the bleeding. She tutted, coming over and pulling my hand away.

"Come with me," she murmured, leading me into one of the bathrooms.

I sat on the edge of the copper bathtub, watching her soak a cloth in water and dab gently at the injury. She took my hands next, cleaning the grazes across my knuckles and binding them with fresh bandages. She was usually the one that tended to me until healers came, and had become something of a friend, though not as close as Catalin and I had become, even though she was much older than me. Being the newest member of the harem, Natalia was also the lowest ranked. Gheata clearly considered me the most demeaning task to be done in the hareem, so I was Natalia's problem.

"I don't think we need to call the healer for these," she murmured, peering at my other hand before wrapping it as well. "Anything else?"

I winced, pulling up my shirt and peering over my shoulder into the mirror.

"Scratch that," Natalia sighed as the blue and black bruise that covered a large portion of my back came into view. "What in Mircia was that?"

"A tree," I mumbled, shimmying the top painfully back down.

Natalia shooed me back out of the bathing room, asking a servant to fetch the healer before pouring tea for us both.

I breathed the fragrant steam in, letting it warm my lungs before taking a sip. It burned comfortably down, helping the bone-deep ache that seemed to resonate through my entire body as I slipped gingerly into a seat.

Natalia busied herself with her tea, moving the paper and ink she had been working on to the side. She was a gifted artist, being able to turn plain, coarse paper and black ink into intricate images, mixing landscape with the beautiful creatures that roamed through it. Every swirl and line seemed to hide some new creature, peeping out from behind a tree or coasting through a cloud and I leaned over to admire it.

"This is beautiful," I said fascinated by her creation.

Natalia hummed, taking a sip of her tea as she turned the page to look at it. "It's ok, I can't get the saybre right, the body is off."

I glanced up at her, her face was tighter than it usually was as if she was distracted by something.

"What?" I asked cautiously, glancing around. It was usually Gheata's presence that gave her that look.

"Hmmm?" She blinked up at me, looking confused.

"What›s wrong?"

Her face tightened further, and she shrugged slightly, though she fidgeted nervously with the carved design of her cup.

"Natalia?"

"I'm pregnant," she breathed. Frowning slightly, her gaze fixed on the murky liquid in her mug.

I reached automatically across the table, unsure of what to say. She raised her eyes to mine, sadness in them. "Surprise!"

I shook my head. "I'm sorry."

Natalia just nodded, turning back to her drawing.

Darius interrupted the silence a while later, striding into the room. He was still pissed with me, I guessed, from the way he wouldn't quite meet my eye.

"Catalin." He bowed to the woman as she emerged from her rooms. "Natalia."

The two women ducked their heads at him as he came to a halt beside me.

"The healer is too busy to attend to you up here, I am to take you down to her," he said bluntly.

I nodded, ignoring the hand he offered to rise. I took far too much satisfaction in hearing his annoyed hiss as I strode past him, stopping in my room to switch out the soft slippers I wore for boots.

I followed him through the halls. I did not often get to come to the lower levels as we usually took the direct route to the courtyard from the harem. My sire had a wing to himself on the far side of the castle. I had heard a bit about it from the women in conversation, after their trips to his quarters. This area, in the middle of the castle, was where his sons resided, as well as the Drayvn held in esteem by my sire, some had entire living quarters here with their own small harems, not that I had ever met any of them.

"Can you slow down?" I hissed at Darius, nearly trotting to keep up with his long strides.

He didn't answer, but checked his pace slightly, letting me draw alongside him.

"Why are you so mad at me?" I murmured, keeping my voice low as servants and Drayvn passed us in the hallways.

"You were a fool today," he muttered, sliding his hands into his pockets. He glanced down at me. "He only wanted to reassure himself you were progressing, you showed him how far you have come in such a short time. Now he will expect harsher training for you."

I blinked at him, taking this information in. I tried to ignore the small glow in my chest at the backhanded compliment, but it was his other words that stuck with me, and I tried to make sense of why as we continued in silence.

The healer answered on the first knock as we reached the lower level, wiping her hands on a bloodstained cloth as she waved us into the dimly lit space. The rooms had...a strong scent of blood and herbs to them. A fireplace crackled in the corner with a copper pot sitting over the flames, metal implements sticking out of the boiling water.

"Sit." She waved a hand to a fur-covered bench in front of the fireplace. "I will be with you momentarily."

She unhooked the pot from over the flames, disappearing through a smaller door with it. I could hear voices murmuring on the other side, a woman's voice rising above the others, hoarse with pain as she gave a low, rolling cry and then silenced to panting.

The healer emerged again, motioning me to take my shirt off with a flick of her fingers.

I did, very aware of Darius› presence in the room, turning my back to him and crossing my arms in front of my chest. It's not that I had much to look at, and now that the harem's fire ran constantly, the women in it had taken to wearing near scandalous clothes that you could make out every dip and curve of beneath. I had seen Darius eyeing them surreptitiously several times, especially Catalin, whose beauty outshone everyone else in the harem, except maybe Gheata, though her personality overshadowed it.

But still, it was my body, and I did not want him to see it.

The healer ran cool hands across my back, the deep ache in it melting away in moments.

"You had four cracked ribs," she said, sounding slightly surprised. "I wouldn't have picked that from how easily you were moving."

"Pain is just temporary, you can ignore it," I murmured, shrugging my shirt back on.

The healer huffed, "Try telling that to some of these young women," she muttered, turning me to peer into my face. She ran a thumb across a tender patch on my eyebrow, her watery eyes scanning me as she did.

"That all?"

I nodded, flexing my neck to and fro. "I think so."

She patted me on the shoulder, glancing back to the half-open door as the woman inside it began to pant again, a low moan of pain breaking out between the pants.

Darius moved towards me, murmuring his thanks to the woman and catching my elbow to lead me away.

I caught a glimpse through the door as we passed it. A young woman, not much older than me by looks was kneeling on a blood-soaked bed, her head hanging low as she rocked slowly. One hand was pressed to the swell of her stomach, kneading the side of it gently as another groan ripped from her.

She was cut off from view as we crossed the room, and I felt Darius' hand tighten on my arm as he too must have seen her.

"She belongs to Kalias harem," he murmured as we slipped from the pungent room. "He was expecting a male from her since the pregnancy has been harsh, she is not due for another month though."

"Hopefully she passes it and survives," I mutter, my spine stiffening.

"You mean hopefully the child survives?" he corrected.

"No," I said through clenched teeth as Natalia slipped through my mind. "If it's male, I hope it>s stillborn, it's the only way she will live through that process."

His hand tightened on my arm painfully. "Don't let them hear you say such things, Little One," he murmured, his lips so close to my ear I could feel his warm breath stir my hair. "Kalias is not one to take a slight like that without punishment."

I yanked my arm from his grip, scowling at him.

I trailed him back through the halls, barely looking where I was going and nearly walked straight into his back as he halted suddenly.

I stepped back from him, sighing in exasperation and then noticed who he had ducked a short bow to.

My ears hollowed out. The breath rushed from my lungs as if I had been punched in the stomach as I felt the clutch on my Drayvn blood slip slightly, the beast inside me cracking an eye open.

"Well, are you not a pretty little flower, cleaned up as you are," Andrei said in that cold, flat voice that had haunted my nightmares all these months.

Such a pretty little flower, so delicious. Mama's soft eyes swam through my mind, how panicked they had been in her final moments. *Lyrik, run.* Papa's unseeing eyes as I tried to hold his neck together.

He grinned at me, his dark eyes glinting as he turned his head to Kalias. I had not noticed him by his side, all my attention was honed on Andrei.

"Is our sister a mute?" he asked casually.

"She had a decent tongue on her the last time I saw her," Kalias said quietly. He was standing stiffly, his body half turned to me, and I realised my body had lowered itself, coiling ready for an attack, a low rumbling snarl building in my chest.

Andrei tutted, his head cocking to the side. "Don't tell me you are still mad about our last altercation. That's the Sylvyn blood in you, such a weakness, Sister."

"It wasn't weak when my teeth were in your neck," I hissed. I didn't even recognise my voice, it sounded hollow, cold in a way I had never heard it. I sounded like them. I felt my claws slip out, felt the ache of my fangs lengthening and watched him tracking my movements as I closed the space between us.

His face hardened. "Try it again, and see what happens," he murmured, so low only I could hear him, as close as I now was.

I welcomed the cool, hollowness that settled over me. My mind went clear, my heart slowed from its frantic beat to a low, steady thump as my eyes went to the pulse in his neck, the beat of it matching my own.

I struck, a snarl ripping out of me as I lunged for him. I would kill him. This is what I had been waiting for, what I had endured these months of training and strengthening my body for. I would kill him and then I would go join Mama and Papa in the land of the oGds.

I'm coming, my heart whispered to them. *Wait for me.*

My teeth snapped in mid-air as rough hands slammed me into the rock wall. A warm body crushing me against the stone.

Lights flickered in my vision at the impact, my ears ringing.

I slammed my head back, connecting with whoever had me and I heard a muffled curse before my head was violently cracked back onto the wall.

"Get a hold of yourself." It was Darius› voice. His mouth was close to my ear, body crushing me so hard I was immobilised.

I heard scuffling and saw Kalias dragging Andrei back against the far wall, out of the corner of my vision.

"You think you would win that?" Darius hissed at me. "What do you expect to gain from that? Even if you maim him, you still have the other to deal with, as well as every other Drayvn in this castle."

"I don't care about any other Drayvn as long as I kill him," I snarled, fighting against Darius› grip.

My heart was beginning to speed up again, pain flickering through the numbness, edged with a wave of murderous anger.

"Let me go, Darius!"

He shoved me again, the breath rushing out of me as he leaned in, the warmth of his cheek against my ear.

"If revenge is what you want, this is not how you get it." It was so low I could barely hear it. I stilled beneath his grip, my heart racing. "Control yourself." He snapped, slightly louder. "And I will let you go."

I paused for a moment, before giving a short, jerky nod. The best I could do pressed up to the wall as I was.

His weight moved away so suddenly I would have crumpled to the floor had he not had the scruff of my shirt fisted in his grip. He shook me, like a disobedient puppy.

"Apologies, My Lords," he faced Andrei and Kalias. "She is still learning to control her temper; it gets away with her sometimes. It's the Sylvyn blood, emotions run strong."

Kalias had a similar grip on Andrei, whose eyes were narrowed on me, his lip curled in a snarl.

"I can see that," Kalias said cooly. "Come, Brother." He moved slightly, putting himself between Andrei and me. "You would not want to gain Father's distrust by killing his new pet so soon."

Darius transferred his grip to my neck, digging his nails in in warning as I tensed. Pulling me back against him as Kalias moved by, pushing Andrei ahead of him.

Andrei and I locked eyes momentarily. A silent conversation in those brief moments. *This is not over.*

Darius hauled me along the corridor, his brutal grip on my neck making my bones creak. We were well out of earshot of Kalias and Andrei before he slammed me back into the wall. I gasped at the impact, my already throbbing head spiking in pain.

"What was that?" He snapped. "You refuse to shift all these months, and then that…"

I glared at him, hating that my eyes were watering from the ache in my head.

"Oh, you do *not* get to go mute on me now. What… have you got a death wish? Kalias would have killed you if you had gotten your teeth into Andrei, you would not have made it out of that hallway. You are fifteen and untrained, Lyrik."

"I don't give two shits if I live or die," I snapped, shoving his chest. He didn't even move against the impact of it, and I gritted my teeth scowling up at him. "You think I want to go on living here? What is left for me, Darius? Get the shit kicked out of me by you every day, and then what's waiting for me is even worse. To be treated like those women in the harem? Spit out children to be raised like those *monsters*? No. I will not do it. But his life is *mine*. I will kill him for what he took from me, and then I will go to the land of the Gods and escape this place."

Darius surveyed me for a moment, his eyes narrowed on my face. "You are smarter than that, Lyrik."

I stiffened, baring my teeth at him.

"You want revenge for your parents. I understand that," he said, his voice low. "But he killed them on your sire's orders. We were instructed to only bring you back and kill anyone that was involved. Do you have any idea how hard I had to work to stop Kalias from killing that farmer and his wife, too? You may be bitter at Andrei, but it is Vladimyre that has done this to you."

I was breathing too fast. I felt like no matter how hard I sucked the breaths in, it wasn't reaching my lungs. The ringing in my ears was back too, coldness spreading through my belly.

"Breathe," he said softly, in a voice I hadn't heard from him before. "Lyrik, breathe… There you go." His eyes held mine as I copied his breaths, the panic that had risen in me halting its cold clutch.

"You can take Andrei down," Darius murmured once I was calmer. "I have no doubt you could have done it right there in front of Kalias and I, your strength is far greater than any of them had at your level, and I was withholding just how far you have come from your sire until you fucked that up today. But that would have been it, you wouldn't have survived the rest of them." He gave me a mirthless smile. "But I can teach you to be the weapon they never see coming, and you can take them all down, every single one of them that had a hand in this."

I blinked at him. "What?"

He shook his head, looking exasperated. "You are not the only one they took everything from. My family ruled this land. I am the firstborn son of the firstborn son. Your father sits on my throne, and I grovel to him every day. You want vengeance, but vengeance is sweeter in the long game Little One, trust me. I have been in this game for decades, waiting for the best card to play." He huffed. "I did not expect you to be that card, but here we are."

My mind was swimming with everything he had just told me. He wasn't the lapdog to my sire I had assumed.

"I can't take them down alone," he murmured, "neither can you. But together, we have a chance to make them all pay. You just need to trust me."

I stared at him. "How?"

"I will train you," he replied. "You do everything I tell you to do, exactly how I tell you to do it, and I will make you the weapon that will bring your sire to his knees and my connections to these people will give me the resources to finish the job. He stepped back, holding his hand out to me. "But I cannot do that unless you are prepared to give me everything you have."

I looked at his hand, then up at him. His face was still that cold mask, but there was something in his eyes I hadn't seen before. Hope.

I could stop him. My sire. Stop him from inflicting more pain on anyone else. Any future daughters that came out like me, this broken abomination that didn't fit in anywhere. Mama's face flashed through me again. He had taken her, he had taken them both, they all had. Determination settled over me and I nodded, reaching out and taking Darius' hand, his clasp firm and warm as I looked up into his eyes.

"Teach me everything. Make me the monster they didn't see coming."

Chapter Fifteen

"I need you to shift."

I stared up at Darius, scowling. "No."

He had taken us further from the castle than we had been yet, moving closer to the base of the mountains that loomed behind my sire's immediate estate and made up the harsh backbone of Mircia, snaking along it and dividing the country into two distinct halves.

Darius scrubbed a hand over his face. "Gods save me," he muttered. He took a resigned breath in and held it for a moment, studying me. "Do you trust me?"

"No."

He huffed a laugh. "Clever girl, at least you have learned that." The corner of his lips tucked in. "Do you trust that I want to see your sire fall as much as you do?'

I studied him for a moment. "Yes," I said cautiously.

He nodded, and I flinched as he tapped the side of my temple. "Drayvn think here and only here. It makes them formidable weapons, but they have a weakness. Do you know what that is?"

I shook my head, eyeing his hand as he reached out and tapped my chest. "They do not understand this."

His eyes darkened slightly as he watched me for a moment. "You have both, Lyrik. You can think like a Drayvn. You have the strength and resilience of a Drayvn, yet you have a Sylvyn heart in there as well. You can read your opponents better than they can, understand what they are doing, and why they are doing it. Choosing only one side is like fighting one-handed when you have the ability to fight with both."

My jaw was clenched so hard it hurt and I had to consciously relax it to be able to speak. "I can't. I can't control it when it comes on."

He cocked his head. "Why the Gods do you think we are out here? We have room for you to lose your head and find it again."

The constant fist of anxiety that lived in my belly tightened further, twisting in my guts.

"Darius, I can't." I could hear the edge in my voice. The waver in it irritated me. I refused to let him see my concern.

"If you want to avenge them, you must," Darius said flatly. "Or you can just keep playing his game. You can be his little pet, do your little tricks for him, and maybe you will get strong enough that when your bloods come and he picks the Drayvn he wants to breed you to, if you survive that you just *might* survive the births of your sons. You never know, you could end up the Prima of your own master's harem. *Prima Lyrik* has a ring to it, don't you think?"

I bared my teeth at him. "I will not be in a harem."

"Oh, you will," Darius chuckled. "You think you have any choice in that?" Vladimyre will chain you to a bed if he has to. He did before with your mother and plenty of others before. Don't think you are any different just because you are of his blood."

He wandered away to the horses, pulling his water skin off his saddle and drinking from it. "Or," he continued after he was done. "You can listen to me. You cannot be far off maturing. We can possibly push it out if we keep your diet light and keep your training heavy, but we do not have time for you to do this half-assed." He crossed the space between us, looming over me. "You told me to make you a weapon. Do as you are fucking told, Lyrik, and I will make you the greatest weapon this country has ever seen."

I clenched my fists, resisting the urge to punch him in the face. "What do I do?" I asked through clenched teeth. Clenched— because it was the only thing stopping me from ripping the pulsing artery out of his neck that I could see so clearly as close as he was.

"You shift," he said evenly. "Not a full shift. I need you to learn to settle in the middle. Let it rise enough to calm you, lower your heart rate. Your eyesight, your reflexes, your hearing, all of it will increase while you will still maintain a level of awareness."

I stared at my hands. "How?"

"I haven't got a damn clue," he grinned.

It took a week of going out to that spot before I could even slow the shift enough to register what a midway point felt like. A week of shifting and getting knocked out so rapidly that I wouldn't see it coming. I would wake up on the floor, Darius looming over me with a look of exasperation. "Again," he would say.

Shift, fail, knocked out, rinse, and repeat.

By the end of that week, I was so battered that even the healers would look sideways at Darius when he hauled me into their chambers, half delirious, for them to work on.

It was late into the eighth day when I felt it. I was running my tongue over my fangs, focusing on the feel of them sliding down, the tips of them pricking my tongue as I did. My heart began to slow, the strength flooding into my limbs was becoming second nature, but that hollow feeling— the feeling that took everything away wasn't there.

I blinked in surprise, my eyes raising to meet Darius'. He was standing across from me, as usual, axe in hand with the blunt end poised to club me when I inevitably lost control.

"Don't do it," I warned him. I could almost see the surprise and delight dance behind his eyes as my vision, so much sharper with my Drayvn senses, picked up the smallest detail, from the small flecks of green in his hazel eyes to the light glinting off the stubble of his face.

"Well done, Little One," he murmured, stepping closer to me.

I could scent him, scent the blood running through his veins. The balm he had used on some ache under his clothing. I could even scent the travel cake he had in his pocket and the leather oil on his hands from the reigns.

"You reek," I hissed at him, my breathing coming ragged as a surge of the shift threatened to tip me over the edge.

"I'm hedging my bets it's not nearly as bad as you did when I met you," he chuckled. I watched his hand reach out, tasting my blood as I bit down on my lip, the pain keeping me grounded in this limbo of two forms. He gently thumbed my lip up, looked at my teeth and nodded his approval. "You have it. Now hold it."

I focused on my breathing, my too-slow heart's sluggish thump in my chest as he circled me.

My leg gave way as he kicked the back of it and I dropped to my knee on the hard ground, grunting at the impact, but still, I held it down. I rolled my head, flexing under the pressure as I got to my feet, clasping my hands behind my back as I regained my position.

"Good girl," he praised, coming into my line of sight again. He feigned towards me, as if to attack, and it took everything in me to keep that rush of emptiness down. I felt the sting as my claws slipped out slightly, digging into my palms.

He stilled a moment as I brought myself under control again, nodding to me as I regained it and began his slow circle again.

I could hear his callouses rasping against the handle of his axe as he hefted it one-handed, distracting me as he gave me a shove. I caught myself easily, breathing.

In— out— in— *Slap.*

Stars exploded across my vision as he slapped me hard across the cheek. The emptiness rushed in as a snarl ripped from my throat.

And then the world went black as the butt of his axe connected with my temple.

"Again."

I sighed, planting my feet with my hands clasped loosely behind my back. Eyeing Darius as he wrapped his hands in cloth strips.

It had been two months since I had managed to find merge— as Darius called it. We had argued for three days over what to call it after his initial offering of, "go mongrel," had nearly lost him his arm. 'Merge' was a truce.

Today, however, was different from our usual training, today my sire was coming to observe again, and we were giving him a show.

We had already moved through the weapons I had been using, allowing Darius to land blows on me that he hadn't gotten close to in months, letting my temper slip here and there.

I watched Darius as he circled me, feigning jabs here and there, letting him get close enough to make a snatch at me and grasp my arm. I snarled at him as he wrenched me into a hold, one arm wrapped painfully around my neck as his breath tickled my ear. "Let it slip, you are being too controlled," he breathed against the shell of my ear before releasing me.

I fell to the floor, lunging back at him, only for my head to snap back as his fist took me under the chin with a loud crack of my jaw. I shifted, keeping myself barely out of a full transition. Spitting blood on the ground as hollowness took over my chest I lunged, teeth snapping for his neck, his arm, any flesh that got within inches of me.

Darius grunted as his foot slipped on the wet, muddy ground, the mistake costing him the precious seconds it took me to sink my fangs into his shoulder. He roared as I bit down, one of my fangs grating against bone.

Claws dug into the back of my neck, wrenching me from him. I hissed and spat blood at my assailant.

Vladimyre just slapped me across the face, shaking me enough to make my teeth clack together painfully. "That will do," he drawled. "I will not have you killing my Secundar."

I hissed at him, spitting like a wildcat in his grip.

Darius stalked towards us, his face set in a scowl.

"Apologies, sire, the ground is wet underfoot."

"Hmmm," Vladimyre said, sounding unimpressed. "She has no better control over it than she had months ago. Maybe what I want to see from her is not obtainable… and this." He shook me again. "This bloodlust she falls into is from repressing her Drayvn instincts like she has been doing."

Darius reached out, his large hand enclosing around my neck as he took me, still snarling under my breath at Vladimyre. "She has moments," he said, shrugging. "I'm sure she has more to give."

Vladimyre made a noncommittal noise in the back of his throat, wiping his hand on his pants.

"If you will excuse us, a dunk in the lake usually gets her back out of it," Darius said, his hand tightening around my neck as I snarled at him.

Vladimyre nodded, waving a hand in dismissal. "Go, I have work to do anyway. Come to my offices tonight, I need you to oversee a few things for me."

Darius bowed his head. "Of course."

I could hear the hooves of my sire's horse loping away, the vibrations under my feet slowly fading as he hauled me in the direction of the lake.

It wasn't until the birds began to sing again that I straightened, brushing the dirt off my clothes.

"That was fucking unnecessary," Darius muttered, releasing me and peering down the torn hem of his collar.

I licked his blood off my teeth and gave him a wicked smile. "You *told* me to slip. Wasn't my fault you stepped in horse shit; he would have noticed if I had pulled back."

He glared at me darkly, refusing to talk again until we got to the lake.

I perched on a rock, holding his shirt for him as he leaned over the cold, dark waters, washing the blood off his skin that had run down under his clothes, and muttering obscenities at me under his breath.

"Do you think he suspects anything?" I asked, watching with an odd feeling as his muscles bunched and flexed as he shrugged back into his shirt.

"You were very convincing," he said, an edge to his voice.

I laughed softly and folded my arms. "Hey, I was being nice to you, you exposed your neck twice."

His head popped through the collar of his shirt, loose hair mussed and his eyes dark. "I did *not*," he snapped.

"You did," I licked my lips. "Lucky for you, I fed this morning."

He grimaced at me as he reached up to bind his hair back. "There is something really wrong with you, you know that right?"

I nodded, giving him a smile that was all fang. "I'm aware."

CHAPTER SIXTEEN

Age Sixteen

"Oh, come onnnnnnn," I teased, looking at Natalia upside down from where I reclined on one of the day beds. Reached out, tugging on the end of her plait. "Just one song."

Natalia gave me a dark look, curling her legs under her skirts and throwing a slice of an apple at me, it rebounded off my forehead with a dull slap.

I snorted, rolling onto my stomach and taking a closer look at the picture she had been drawing. It was a portrait of Emala, one of the women that had passed last month. She had captured the woman perfectly, the proud tilt of her chin, the tattoos down her brow.

"Gorgeous," I murmured, stealing the rest of her apple slices. "But you still haven't given me the song you promised."

"*You* promised you would describe the waterfall you went to last month for me to draw," Natalia quipped, tapping me on the end of the nose with her quill.

I grinned at her. "It was very wet."

Natalia rolled her eyes at me. "Why do you have to turn *everything* filthy."

I sat up, feigning outrage. "I do *not!* I was being literal."

Natalia hummed noncommittally, turning her attention back to her drawing.

"You are here later than usual?" Catalin said, smiling warmly as she glided into the room. I was slightly jealous of the effortless way she moved, she looked as if she were made of water, gliding across the floor with such fluidity that it looked as if she were always a moment away from dancing. Not even the three-month bulge of pregnancy detracted from it.

"Darius said he would collect me when he was ready to leave," I said, waving my hand at her. "I think he was getting his sword mended first."

Catalin gestured to Natalia to lean in as she blew her tea, wiping a smudge of kohl from under the woman's eye. She patted her cheek gently when she was done. "Beautiful," she murmured.

The two of them had gotten closer than they were in the previous year, Natalia having withdrawn into a depression so deep that we all thought her lost after the birth of her daughter not even a year ago. Only the combined effort of me keeping Gheata away from her, and Catalin throwing all her energy into the woman had kept her going after the child was taken from her arms, still on her childbed. The echo of her smile had begun to emerge, and she had begun to sing in her beautiful voice.

We all looked up as the heavy doors swung inward, and Darius strode in. He had become more relaxed in these quarters, knowing that no other male would be permitted here, it stopped the risk of any of my brothers or sire catching him in conversation with the women, and Gheata was not hard to avoid. Being the only woman permitted to roam freely, she was rarely in the harem aside from mealtimes and for the checks she still did on me.

"Ready?" He asked, smiling at Catalin and Natalia as he approached us. He peered over Natalia›s shoulder at her picture, keeping a respectful distance between them. "That is magnificent," he said, nodding to the picture as she glanced up at him.

She flashed him a small smile.

Catalin gathered her skirts around her legs to get up and I felt my brows nearly touch my hairline in surprise as Darius reached a hand to help her up. Secundar or not, if he was caught touching one of my sire's harem, he would be brutally punished, if not killed outright. I had seen a servant beheaded after bumping one of the wives after tripping on a rug. There was no excuse.

Catalin let him haul her upright and murmured her thanks before excusing herself and hurrying off to the washroom. This pregnancy had plagued her with morning sickness that tended to be all-day sickness. I had stayed up with her many nights, wiping her brow with a damp cloth and quietly telling her about my days with her head in my lap.

He raised a brow at me, "Ready?" He asked again, drawing the word out and sounding slightly irritated.

"Yes yes," I muttered, flouncing to my feet. "Don't get your britches in a twist."

I heard his muttered retort as I passed him and flipped him off for it behind my back.

"*Lyrik!*" Natalia breathed, mortified.

I spun, walking backwards towards my room and blew her a kiss.

I grabbed my cloak and boots from my room, lacing the sturdy things onto my feet and tucking my stolen daggers into the sides of them. I wasn't permitted my weapons up here; Darius always kept them in his rooms. I had stolen these daggers from him not long after he had made his confession to me, nearly eighteen months ago, and if he had noticed I had them, he turned a blind eye to it.

He wandered in as I was shrugging into my cloak, and chuckled as he took in the padded britches and multiple layers of shirts and tunics I had covered myself with.

"Padding?"

"Cold," I muttered. I barely had an ounce of fat on me, all lean muscle that moved under my skin, but it made me feel the cold more than I ever had before.

"Pussy," he mocked.

"Jerk," I threw back, stretching to check I could actually move with the constricting clothes. "Please tell me nothing with water today? It will take ages to get these off." I hadn't quite forgiven him yet for the hypothermia I had endured after forcing me to submerge in the frozen lake for hours at a time.

He told me it was to gain better control of the merge, work through the pain, blah blah blah. I thought he was a masochist who got some form of sick pleasure watching me float around like a pissed-off ice cube while cursing him, his mother, and his mother's mother with every foul word I had picked up over the years.

It had just won me a black eye.

"No water," he snorted, sucking on a tooth. "Your sire has asked me to go retrieve the taxes from some unwilling homesteads on the outskirts. Andrei is still not back yet, and Kalias has other matters to attend to. You are to come with me."

I sighed, "again?"

"Quit your whinging and pack a bag."

Clenching my teeth, I grabbed the nearest pack and stuffed some clothing into it, picking the warmest pieces I had. The last trip to collect taxes had been within Corvin's borderlands and I had seen things I hoped to never see again. My sire's version of a second chance was the loss of a body part. In this case, it was the farmer's wife's eye.

With the longest winter Mircia had on record, it seemed no one could afford their taxes, even with the knowledge of the risks.

Darius had ordered me to hold the woman. I had refused, he had broken two of my ribs and fractured my arm. I still had to watch as her eye was removed, refusing to merge and take some of the horror away for myself. She deserved that respect at least, for someone to bear witness. The vomiting I had done afterwords had displaced one of my ribs and I had coughed blood the entire ride back until I could get to a healer.

Darius and I had argued bitterly after that. I had accused him of being more of a pawn to my father than he realised. He told me my weakness would ruin everything we had been working towards. What was one woman's eye, when we could liberate a country.

I shouldered my pack sullenly and jerked my chin at the door waiting for him to lead the way. Trying not to imagine what horrors the next few days would entail. I had been irritated all day, my temper shorter than my usual already short fuse, and if I were honest, I wanted to pick a fight with him to work off the pent-up aggression.

We both came to a halt in the doorway as Gheata loomed in front of us, her usual scowl extra sour this morning.

I gave her the overly sweet smile that I knew irked her, watching as the muscle in her jaw clenched.

"Yesterday›s clothes?" She asked.

"I'm wearing them," I said with a mocking grin. "It's snowing out there and my ass gets cold." I held a finger up, ferreting around in the back pocket of my pants. "Oh wait, I did have these for you though."

I hooked my discarded underwear out, dangling them from a finger and waggled my brows at her before flicking them across the space between us. "There you go panty sniffer, all yours."

Darius gave a strangled cough, striding past the woman.

Gheata threw my offering on the floor with a disgusted sound, pointing her long finger at me.

"The day you leave this harem, I will rejoice."

I patted her on the shoulder as I passed, pausing to look directly into her face. "Girl. Same."

I caught up to Darius before he hit the stairs to the lower levels. He seemed to have regained his composure slightly.

"You shouldn't bait her like that," he murmured to me as we took the stairs two by two.

"Why?" I chuckled. "It's the highlight of my day."

"She has your sire›s favour," Darius warned.

"It's been two years almost to the day, Darius," I sighed. "If she could have done something about me, she would have done so approximately one year and eleven months ago."

Darius huffed. "Can't say I blame her. You are insufferable."

"I aim to please," I said, giving him a bright smile.

We rode out from the castle in silence. Darius, quiet even for him led the way, my horse falling into step with his as it usually did.

"Quite the conversationalist today, aren't you?" I prodded, eyeing him warily.

He gave me a black look. "Do not start."

"Oh good, it's going to be one of those kinds of days," I muttered, twisting in the saddle to ease the dull aching in my lower back and stomach. "How *far* are we going? At least tell me that?"

"Coastal town off the south coast," he replied shortly.

"Coastal town off the south coast," I mocked, replicating his deep, rough voice as best I could— oh, I was really pushing it. "That's super informative. I'm hungry, did you bring snacks?"

I caught the wrapped bundle of dried meat that he lobbed over his shoulder with one hand, laughing softly and tucked into it, chewing on the salty meat.

We rode for the rest of the day in relative silence, every attempt I made at pushing him into the easy conversation we usually had and that I had grown accustom to, failing miserably. Even after we had picked a camp for the night on the banks of a mountain stream, he disappeared off into the forest around us without a word as I unpacked the bed rolls, coming back well over an hour later with a fat pheasant to cook over the fire. He offered me the blood in its veins, but one sniff of it told me it had already cooled too much for my liking, and I settled for some of the meat instead, its smoky skin crunchy after slow roasting over the fire.

I took my knives after the meal, setting up small rocks on a log of wood and proceeding to send the knives flying through the air and embedding in the wood beneath each of them in turn.

Thud, thud, thud. Walk over, retrieve. *Thud, thud, thud.*

"Would you stop that," Darius hissed from where he was reclining on his bedroll next to the fire.

"What is up your ass today?" I asked, retrieving my knives and sending them for a third round. "You should be happy I'm training, it's not like you are training me."

I saw the flash of his teeth as he bared them at me across the fire.

"Truth hurts," I quipped, retrieving my knives again. I was just reaching out for my third knife when one of his thudded into the wood beneath my hand, a thin line of blood welling across my wrist where it had nicked it.

"You want to train?" He murmured, stalking up to me. "Fine. We will train. Your cockiness is going to be your undoing, you would do well to remember it."

I merged, running my tongue over my fangs, and smiled at him. "Maybe, but at least I don't spend my days kissing the ass of the man who took my future from me."

I had overstepped, I knew it the moment his face smoothed into a blank canvas. His only tell that rage was overtaking him was the fact that he had no tells, his normal mannerisms disappearing beneath the honed killer he had turned himself into. This was the fight I had been stirring for all day and I snarled at him, baring both my fangs.

He huffed a cold laugh, stepping into my space until I was forced to look up at him. "You think I kiss his ass, Little One," he murmured, his voice smooth and dripping with acid. "Are you jealous? Do you want me to kiss your ass, too?" He reached a finger out, running the cold tip of it along my jaw.

I jolted, stepping back and slipping out of the merge. He never touched me, not unless it was to beat me senseless or restrain me. The feel of it made me instantly uncomfortable.

He narrowed his eyes. "Pathetic. Almost two years of training and you lose your grip on it that easily, then have the balls to accuse me of weakness. Merge."

I did, slipping back into it before the bite of his words could settle in me.

"You act like coming out here and doing these things to *my* people shouldn't affect me. Good to see you are embracing that Drayvn blood of yours after all."

I ignored his words, letting them wash over me. He knew it affected me, he was trying to get me to bite, both literally and figuratively.

"You think it is not escaping me, *Lyrik,* that you are on the cusp of your seventeenth birthday, and you are not ready yet?" he went on, his breath curling in the cold air, inches from my face. "I have put two years into you and for all your cockiness, you are not ready. It is only by the grace of the Gods you have not begun your bloods yet. Which is yet *another* topic your sire is now questioning me on." He gripped my chin between his fingers, turning my face to him. "He thinks it's the training that has delayed it, and he isn't wrong. Do you know how hard I've had to work to get him to agree to continue this arrangement? And then what do I get from you? You ungrateful brat."

His fingers dug painfully into my jaw, but I held my merge, my gaze locked on his.

"I have it under control."

"Do you now?" His fist slammed into my lower stomach and my breath exploded from me, doubling over as I gasped for air. I kept an iron fist on the merge, the pain just a dull ache in the back of my mind as I straightened, settling my feet against the ground and clasping my hands loosely behind my back again.

"I have it *under control.*" My voice was slightly breathy from the blow, but I was comfortable. The merge settled over me like a net.

I tensed for the second blow just below my ribs, barely feeling it as my muscles absorbed the impact and gave him a mocking smile. "Ouch."

He circled me and the brush of his hand across my rear almost made me slip, only an internal lunge, hauling myself back into place kept me from losing it.

He must have noticed, though I don't think I moved as his hand suddenly fisted in my hair, yanking my head back until his cheek was next to mine. "*Do* you have it under control?"

"Yes," I spat at him. I could feel my heart begin to speed, anxiety pushing through my calm senses.

"I don't think you do," he murmured, his free hand curling around me to cup my breast. I hadn't worn a binder for training since my body had lost the slight curves that I had barely begun to get, instead honing into muscle. There was barely anything there to bind anyway, and I hated the feel of them since I had spent years so tightly trussed.

He ran his hand back down my torso, pulling my body against his.

"Darius, what are you doing?" I snarled, trying to yank my hair from his grasp.

"Teaching you a fucking lesson," he hissed.

I barely had control of myself. I was surging between slipping out of merge and spiralling into it, anxiety and anger ripping through me in waves that crashed against each other.

His hand was cold against my skin as he slipped it under my tunic, reaching back up and pinching a nipple painfully.

I lost my grip, the shock of such an intimate touch sent me spiralling so fast down into a shift that it took me a moment to realise what had happened. Long enough that I didn't have time to react, even with my Drayvn blood in full roar, when I was suddenly flying through the air and into the black waters of the river beside us.

The cold hit me like a hammer, throwing me back out of the shift as fast as I had gone into it and I broke the surface, spluttering and coughing up water, my limbs instantly going stiff from the frigid temperature.

I kicked towards the bank; my hair plastered to my face as Darius strolled down its bank in time with me.

He held his hand out to me as I reached him, I ignored it, trying to pull myself out, the layers of sodden clothes dragging me backwards.

"Get away from me," I hissed as he went to grasp my wrist.

He snorted, ignoring my protests and instead grabbed the scruff of my tunic, hauling me out, with what felt like half the river gushing from my clothing.

I wrenched myself from his grip the second my feet hit land, lashing out at his hand that steadied me.

"Don't touch me."

"You needed to see," he said calmly, shrugging out of his cloak and holding it up in front of him.

"See what, that I hate you?"

"See that you need to focus, that there is more we need to work on, and fast. That self-righteous attitude you are getting is only slowing you down."

I scowled at him, beginning to shake so badly from the cold

that I merged to take the edge off of it.

"Get out of those clothes before you get hypothermia again," he said, his voice softening. "I won't look."

He turned his head away, looking out over the water.

I eyed him a moment, but the chill of my sodden clothing was breaking through even the armour of my merge. I shed the clothing in the space of seconds, stepping into the warmth of his cloak that still held the traces of his body heat.

He rubbed his hands up and down my arms, warming me beneath the thick cover. "I apologize for the... shock of that," he said.

It was the first time he had ever apologised to me, and to be honest, I couldn't decide what unnerved me more. I just nodded shortly and crossed to the fire, pulling the cloak tight around myself and letting him deal with my clothing.

Fuck today. And fuck Darius.

I didn't speak to Darius for the rest of the night, wrapping myself in his cloak and curling onto my bedroll. My stomach ached deep inside, a steady dull throb that curled into my lower back. I pulled my legs up, hugging them to me as I mulled over ways to repay him for the punches he had dealt.

I pretended to be asleep as he threw an extra blanket over me later that night, listening to him move around our meagre camp, stoking the fire against the wolves that prowled heavily in these areas. I don't think I even slept most of that night, replaying his hands on me, over and over in my head. I couldn't even begin to understand what it made me feel. Darkest night had long passed when I slipped into merge just to give myself some relief and finally let sleep claim me.

CHAPTER SEVENTEEN

My stomach cramping woke me at dawn. A low ache in my belly where he had punched me. I pushed myself up, stretching cautiously and then froze, the feeling of dampness between my legs coming a second before the scent of blood drifted to me.

"Darius."

My voice sounded thin. As if someone had a hand on my throat, and he spun from where he had been warming water over the fire, hearing the distress in the word.

"What, what's wrong?"

He took a step towards me as I felt the blood drain from my face, holding my hand up in front of me, the tips stained with blood.

He swore viciously as the mortification of what was happening began to settle into me. Heat roared into my cheeks, and I looked around wildly for something, anything to staunch the flow from between my thighs that I could feel now that I had moved.

There was nowhere to disappear to, which I was desperate to do. There weren't even trees around our camp, and I couldn't do anything but just sit there in horror as Darius stalked angrily to the saddle packs.

Ripping fabric jerked my attention back to him as he approached me, tearing one of his shirts into strips.

"Here," he said gruffly. "Go to the river and clean yourself up. I will go for a walk and give you some... space."

I took the strips of cloth from him, nodding stiffly and watched his departing form until he had disappeared around a bend in the river.

I numbly extricated myself from the tangle of blankets and cloak and made my way to the water, gritting my teeth at the ache that rippled across my belly and down through my thighs, and just submerged my lower half back into the frozen water. The cold helped slightly and by the time I got back out, retrieving some clothes from my own packs and working out how to stuff the fabric into them, the ache had subsided somewhat.

I busied myself packing the camp up until Darius returned on silent feet. "I will get you some supplies at the village," he muttered. "There will be women there."

I nodded, feeling the heat rush to my face again. I thought last night had been bad enough, today had barely started and it was significantly worse already.

My mind raced as we saddled up and moved out. Every plan we had had flying out the window. He had said last night I wasn't ready, and now we were out of time. My options were to run and lose the opportunity for the revenge that I had thrown everything into, or stay, and what Darius had done last night would be nothing in comparison to what awaited me back at Cormac once my sire found out I was 'breedable'.

I jumped as Darius› deep voice broke the silence, his horse dropping back to walk alongside mine. "He won't find out. Not this time."

"What?"

He ran a hand over his face, squinting up at the sun. "We won't get to the village until tonight, if that," he muttered. "We can stretch that to tomorrow night if say… your horse throws a shoe and we have to walk it in." He glanced across at me. A day there, maybe two if there is trouble, two days back, riding slowly because your horse is lame. It will be over before we get back, and he won't scent it on you."

I grasped what he was saying, my chest loosening slightly.

He reigned up, reaching out to pull my horse to a halt too. I can try to get you out of the castle each month, give us a bit more time. But if he finds out…" he drifted off, the concern on his face throwing me off. "He can't know I am keeping it secret."

I clenched my jaw. "You can't scent blood. He won't know you know; I could be hiding it from you too."

He nodded, face stern. "He won't let me continue to train you if he knows. But it doesn't mean we can't continue the plan. It would just complicate things."

I laughed softly, sounding as cold as my sire. "What, you would come to liberate me from my chains."

"If I had to, yes," he said without batting an eyelid. "I will get you clothes to give to Gheata for the trip. We will burn those before we get back."

I grunted in agreement, turning my head away from him so he didn't see the tear that slowly ran down my cheek.

We camped on the outskirts of the village that night. Close enough to see the plumes of smoke that curled lazily into the air from the chimneys. I was too miserable to talk, and the urge to feed had been nagging at me relentlessly. He must have realised what I needed as I hadn't even realised he was gone, buried down into my bedroll as I had been when he returned with a small deer over his shoulders, draining the blood for me to feed on.

"Thank you," I said after I had drunk so much my belly felt

distended. The warmth of it soothed some of the aches in me and calmed my frayed nerves slightly.

"You're welcome," he murmured, cutting up the rest of the meat for his dinner.

"What if I'm not enough?" The question slipped from me without meaning to.

Darius huffed softly. "You will be."

"How are you so certain?"

He looked at me thoughtfully, rolling his neck side to side to loosen the muscles there. "You have something that you cannot train. No matter how hard you try, you can teach someone to fight, to move, to endure. You have all that, yet you have the one thing that I have never been able to teach any of your brothers."

"Emotion?" I scoffed. "How is that going to give me an edge over fighting Drayvn? If anything, it's a weakness. My sire wants it to fight Sylvyn, not other Drayvn."

"Not emotion," Darius murmured. "Instinct. You are a killer, Lyrik. I have never trained anyone with as much natural instinct as you have, and it is entirely tied to the emotion you have as a Sylvyn. You shouldn't be nearly the level you are in the limited time I have been able to train you."

I wasn't sure if I felt warm from the blood, or if it was apprehension creeping over me, so I just nodded, staring at the empty cup in my hands.

"I'm not saying we can win," he said, his voice still gentle But I will be right there with you, Little One. Win or lose, we will do it together."

Something squeezed in my chest, and I looked up at him. "We will win," I said. Willing it to be true.

We rode into the village the following morning. We didn't get a warm greeting, people shrank from us as we rode past their houses, heading for our destinations.

The first house we stopped by was straightforward, the farmer had sold one of his horses and fronted up with his taxes on the spot, only earning himself a broken nose for his late payment. The next house, however, did not go so well.

It was a young couple, still new to taking their farm over and owing an entire year in taxes. The male, a tall brutish looking Sylvyn with water gifts was sullen and argumentative, his wife, a small pretty thing shrinking back against the walls of their cottage as we entered.

"I haven›t got it," the man said, tugging on one of his pointed ears. "Take one of the pigs as payment."

"One pig won›t even cover half of what you owe," Darius sneered, his hands sitting loosely in his pockets. "How about I just kill you and sell the farm, problem solved."

The man's eyes flared. "No no, no need for that." He glanced around, his eyes flitting over everything in his house before they fell on his wife. "Here," he said, hauling her forward by a wrist. "Why don't you take her out to the shed for a bit."

I snarled at him, "You would whore your own wife for your debts?"

The man shrugged. "Aint no difference to me now is it. Honest work."

He stumbled back as my fangs slid down and I advanced a step on him, stopping only when Darius' hand rested on my shoulder.

"I am not in the habit of bedding women without their consent," Darius said, his voice cool. "And regardless, you owe the taxes to his Lordship, not me."

"Then take her back for his harem, she›s a good girl, does what she's told, that should cover me for at least the ye—" he cut off in a strangled scream as I launched for him, my claws raking down his face. One manoeuvre had me behind him and his neck snapped, my anger at the last few days unleashing on him.

"Oh, for fucks sake," Darius sighed as the man dropped, limp at my feet. "Did you have to?"

"He›s a pig and deserved it," I muttered.

His wife was crushed against the wall, panting in fear as I turned to her. I put my hand out to her, pulling back quickly as she screamed in terror.

"Stop that," Darius muttered, shooing me out of the way. He took a deep breath and held both hands out to her, placatingly. "We don't want to hurt you," he said cautiously. "But you know your husband owed a good sum of money to the lord. From what I've seen, there is not much here to sell other than the farm itself, which if you do, will repay what he owed and leave you with a tidy sum for a small cottage somewhere." He snapped his fingers in the air in front of her, making her attention drag from her husband›s corpse to him. "I do not want to come back here and have to hurt you, understand?"

She nodded jerkily. "Th-thank you," she said in a small voice. "He was not a good man."

"Shocking," Darius said dryly. "Do you have someone who can help you sell the land? I will need to see the taxes repaid by next quarter."

She nodded again. "My Da will help me."

"Good." Darius straightened, turning to leave, but paused, his face taking on a resigned look. He turned back to the woman, looking slightly awkward as he ran a hand over the back of his neck. "Do you have... women supplies I can purchase from you... and maybe some clothing?"

CHAPTER EIGHTEEN

The following two farms we visited went easily. This time, no more torture was inflicted as the men in question had managed to sell, borrow, and most likely steal to gather the taxes together ahead of our visit.

We stayed in the village that night, Darius securing rooms for us at the one inn the town had. Two dusty, cramped rooms that I was certain were filthier than sleeping out on the ground, but it was definitely warmer.

I rolled my bedroll out on top of the rough pallet, not wanting to risk the stained blankets that were stretched out on the makeshift bed. I noticed, with no small amount of humour, that Darius had done the same when I went to close my door.

We rode out the next day, keeping a leisurely pace as we picked our way over the countryside.

Darius was still off with me, had been so since our fight, and it was making me uneasy. It didn't get any better when it started to rain, both of us riding in sodden, unhappy silence through the day. It wasn't until late afternoon that the rain eased, and the sun crept out from behind the clouds, warming me and beginning to dry the clothes that had been stuck to my skin uncomfortably for hours.

It did nothing to lighten the black mood Darius was in, and he announced we would make camp for the night.

This part of the countryside had barely any cover, most of it being rocky, craggy terrain with minimal trees. When we came across a small copse of trees that provided at least a hint of shelter, we set to arranging our accommodations for the evening.

Darius built a fire and unpacked the camp while I unsaddled and hobbled the horses and quickly wiped them down.

He had the fire crackling by the time I was done, and I gratefully lowered myself next to it, sitting close enough that my still-damp clothes began to steam.

"You are not strong enough to take them all together, even with us both."

The comment pulled me out of the trance I had been in, staring at the flames.

"What?"

"We have months, if that, before Vladimyre finds out," he said quietly. "I know he is already contemplating who he will breed you to, and months is not enough to be the difference in a win on strength alone, as I was hoping. We need to be strategic with how this plays, or this has been a monumental waste of time."

My lip curled in disgust at how nonchalant his words were.

"I will not be 'bred' to anyone."

"You will, if we do not do this correctly," he said flatly. "I was planning to make a move within the next six months, but if we have to bring the timeline forward, so be it."

I blinked at him.

"You didn't tell me you were planning already."

"I have been planning since the second I realised your potential," he huffed, skewering hunks of deer meat on a sharpened stick.

"There is only one way to do this, and that is to take them each out separately. Strongest first and then my men can clear the castle and fortify the surrounding area. Stop any Drayvn that would answer a call for aid if they do get one out. Vladimyre needs to be first because if he is alerted, neither of us will best him."

"And how do you propose I get him off guard?" I asked through my teeth.

"The one place he will least expect it," Darius said. He had the decency to look at least slightly apologetic as he murmured his next words.

"You will take the place of one of his wives."

"WHAT?" I sprang up, disgust overwhelming me. "I will *not.*"

"Not in *that* way," he sighed, motioning me to sit down again. I ignored it, glaring at him.

"*Only* his concubines are permitted in his rooms," he explained. "Not even servants are allowed in there, he is a smart man and knows that is where he is vulnerable. I have learned the layout, and the practices that go on behind those doors, and there is no way for me to get in there. However, I accompany his choice to his wing and let her through the doors most nights. I could get you in, but that is where my involvement would end."

"You don't think he will get suspicious with me waltzing through his doors, knives in hand?" I asked sarcastically.

"Of course, he will," Darius said, his tone turning colder. "But he is held late many nights and he would not be suspicious of his wife falling asleep waiting for him in his bed."

My jaw hurt from clenching it.

"There is no other way to get him close enough to you, unarmed and unsuspecting," he said. "I'm taking as much of a risk as you. I will be guarding his doors and letting him in. If you do not succeed, he will know I have betrayed him and the next neck he will rip out will be mine."

"It feels like the greater risk is falling on my neck and not yours, *Darius*," I spat at him. "Why don't you put a dress on and warm his bed yourself."

He just glared at me blankly.

I breathed heavily through my nose, pacing along the edge of the camp.

"You could have run years ago. You chose this."

His words made me freeze, my eyes narrowing on him.

"Don't deny it," he said softly. You have been able to best me for at least a year. You could have slipped from me a lot sooner than that. If you wanted to run, you would have. You want revenge, I'm giving it to you. Stop being a child and throwing a tantrum about the method by which we achieve this. You think I have not tried to think of every possible way to do this?"

"And what are you getting from this?" I snapped, throwing my arms wide. "You are so desperate to help because of the slight against your family, what are you going to achieve when they are gone."

"Freedom," he barked back, his temper rising. "I can take my fucking life back and go *wherever* the hell I want. Do you think I *want* to be Vladimyres› lapdog? I can't even take a woman without his approval."

He got up, stalking around the fire until he towered over me. "You have lived nearly seventeen years, fourteen of those in relative comfort with parents that loved you and freedom to do what you pleased. I have seen fifty-one years, and in every fucking one of them I have been in service to a man I detest. If he says jump, I have to say how high?"

"How awful for you," I hissed at him. "At least you are worth more than cattle to him. Because that's the entire sum of my existence, livestock in a fun experiment to entertain him. And if you call me a child again, I will show you exactly how well I can now *best* you, Darius." I let the merge take over, my voice dropping to the deadly hiss of the Drayvn as I spat the last words at him.

He just smiled at me, a cold mirthless smile, as his eyes ran blatantly down my chest.

"No, I guess you are not a child anymore, are you," he murmured.

I snarled at him, pushing past him back to the fire and the meat that was now slightly burnt sitting over its flames, trying to ignore the way that his gaze raking down my body made me feel.

Did I even know how it made me feel?

I slept on the far side of the fire to him that night, waking at first light to bathe in the frigid river. I didn't care, the need to feel clean outweighed the bite of the water. Women's bloods were an annoyance. Messy, uncomfortable, and just irritating and I was relieved to see it was already passing.

Darius was bent over my horse's hoof when I returned to camp.

"What are you doing?" I asked as I saw him prying her shoe off. "We are still two days from the Corvin."

"We run the risk of passing scouts that will report back to Vladimyre this close to Corvin," he muttered. "It's bad enough, I don't want to damage her to make her limp, losing a shoe will have to do. I can at least say she was lame at first, and it came right off without you riding her. You can ride with me the rest of the journey."

I swore under my breath, and he chuckled softly. If nothing else, I was at least slightly relieved he seemed to be getting his sense of humour back.

A while later, I looked up at the hand Darius held down to me.

"Can I not just ride behind you?"

"Trust me, it would be even less comfortable than riding in front of me with my swords and the pannier bags on my saddle," he sighed, "Would you just get up."

I sighed, gripping his forearm as his hand curled around my wrist and hoisted me effortlessly into the saddle in front of him.

He passed me the reigns for my own mare, letting me lead her as he steered his gelding one-handed on the other side of me.

I tensed as his free arm wrapped around my middle, holding me against him, his warmth against my back was so unusual. Riding was even worse. The gentle rocking against his body made my face flame, I merged just to take the edge off it, sitting stiffly in front of him as I tried to think of anything other than the man at my back.

"I take it you are hungry?" Darius chuckled as my stomach grumbled loudly against his arm.

It was well-passed midday, and my stomach was trying to claw its way out, but I shrugged anyway.

He reached back, fumbling in one of his saddle bags and came back with an apple, handing it to me. His hand moved to my waist, resting there, leaving my arms free to eat with and I had to force every bite of that apple down as dry as my mouth had suddenly gone.

As big as his hands were against me, his thumb nearly reached to my spine, his fingers curling all the way around my side to my stomach, the gentleness of them something I was completely unused to. For the next hour I retreated back into my thoughts, trying to make sense of how my body was reacting to that touch.

I felt warm and cool at once, my skin so sensitive against my clothing that it was distracting and I had to pull my tunic away from my chest a few times, the rub of it against my breasts uncomfortable.

I gave up trying to hold onto a merge and slipped out of it entirely, welcoming the dulling of his scent that came with the lesser senses of my Sylvyn form. I hadn't remembered him smelling so... pleasant before.

It was a relief as night began to dim the sky above, and once we picked a camp I beelined for the river while he set up, to take a very long, very cold swim.

CHAPTER NINETEEN

"I have those clothes for you in the far saddle bags, everything you are wearing and have worn needs to be burnt before we leave this morning."

I nodded, walking over to where he had gestured and pulling the clothes out. They were similar enough to the clothes I usually wore, but Gheata was nothing if not observant.

I dressed quickly behind a patch of bushes, bringing mine back out and throwing them on the fire. "These are far too clean," I said, glancing down at the clothing in dismay. "There is no way I would be this clean after a week of travelling.

"Your right," Darius mused, strolling up to me and eyeing my clothing critically.

I only registered the glint in his eyes seconds before the handful of mud hit me straight in the chest.

"Ugh!" I stared down at myself, blinking at the wet slop that was sluggishly running down my chest. "You prick!"

He just reached a finger out, swiped it through the mud and then flicked his finger across my nose. "There. Filthy," he teased.

I glared at him, but I was quietly relieved to see the warmth of humour cross his features again.

"There is still a days' ride ahead of us, so plenty of time for you to get dirty," he chuckled, turning to strap the last of the camp items onto my horse.

He hoisted me onto his horse, vaulting up behind me, and we settled back into an easy loping stride, my horse bumping into our legs every now and then.

The landscape had begun to turn more to the forests that stretched out from Corvin and the occasional howl of a wolf echoed through the trees.

It was around midday that my bladder started protesting, the burbling river we followed not helping. I tried to ignore it, shifting in the saddle trying to relieve the pressure.

"Stop wriggling," Darius said after a while, his hand moving to my hip and squeezing.

"Sorry," I muttered, "can we stop for a break soon?"

"I want to get to that inn on the outskirts before we break," he said roughly. "I'm dying for an ale."

I nodded. We had come in a different direction than usual, and I couldn't identify where we were from the landscape. I shifted again, rocking back into his chest as my bladder ached.

"Lyrik," Darius hissed, wrapping an arm around my stomach. "Would you stop that?"

The added pressure on my stomach made it worse and I tried to shift back slightly to ease it. He seemed to get it, his arm loosening slightly, and I was able to get a moment's relief.

Something hard in his clothing was digging uncomfortably into my lower back, as hard up against him as I was, and I slipped my hand between us to push it to the side.

Darius froze.

I froze.

"That is attached," he said in a strained voice.

I don't even know what I would call the noise that came out of me as I swung my leg across the horses whithers and slithered ungracefully to the ground, my knees giving way as I hit the ground and ended up sitting between my own horse's hooves.

My face went hot as he just blinked down at me, his mouth open and one brow raised. I scrabbled to my feet with the little dignity I had left, running for the nearest bush to relieve myself. I had to force myself to come back out, feeling the heat of a blush that crept down my neck.

"You could have just said you needed to stop to piss rather than grope me," he said dryly.

I couldn't look at him as I walked towards him, tying the drawstring of my pants. I took his hand when it appeared in front of me, letting him haul me back onto the horse and sitting stiffly in front of him. There was a noticeable gap between our bodies now and I heard him sigh, grasping my tunic at my hip to hold me.

"It's just a … normal reaction… for a man," he said gruffly. "I asked you to stop wriggling, I thought you understood why."

My ears had started to heat up with the rest of my face and neck, and I knew just how red they must be. It mingled with the heat in my belly that had sparked to life.

"I… sorry," I said, not sure of what else to say, mortification claiming every semblance of sense in me.

"It's fine," he said with a strained laugh. "Should be me apologizing anyway."

We rode in strained silence a while longer, his hand leaving the fabric of my tunic to rest lightly against my hip again. It was invoking all kinds of feelings in me that I struggled to unpack from one another. My traitorous mind kept replaying the moment my hand had closed on his cock.

I jumped guiltily when he spoke again, as if he could see into my mind somehow, his voice rumbling against my back. "We will be back in Corvid tonight, is it uh… safe… to go back? Or do we need another night?"

"It's safe," I replied, my own voice sounding tight. "What do we do next time?"

"I haven't quite figured that out yet," he muttered, adjusting the reigns in his hand. "The only reason he lets me take you with me on these trips is that he knows damn well you would likely end up dead without me there to monitor you, but there is going to be no need for me to leave again until the next quarter."

I swore under my breath.

He huffed. "Yup."

A familiar landmark caught my eye, drawing my attention to it and I scanned the surrounding woods slowly.

"What?" Darius asked, his hand moving to the sword at his side.

"I know these woods," I said hesitantly, leaning to the side to scan the way we had come.

We came to a fork in the rough path we had been following, taking the slightly larger dirt road that looked like it had seen more thoroughfare, and my memory jogged at the hills in the background.

"We are close to my home," I said, eyes now wildly scanning the trees. "I know this road."

Darius swore as again, I slipped my leg over his horse's whithers and jumped down, jogging ahead a way.

"Lyrik," he called, and I could hear the warning in his voice.

"I'm just looking," I called back, seeing the old tree ahead that I had sometimes sat on, waiting for Papa to come home. It was right here! If we carried on this road there would be a right turn down the small dirt road that Mama used to get me to rake, but there was an old track through the trees here that I used to come through as a shortcut.

I spied the tall maple tree that marked the track and broke into a sprint through the trees, hearing Darius curse behind me and call my name again.

Hooves thundered down the road behind me, Darius' voice trailing off as I dipped and curved through the trees, seeing the faint line of the old path that I had walked so many times as a child. I just wanted to see it, wanted to sit on the deck and pretend for one moment I was just waiting for them to come home from the market. Even if the home had new occupants in it now, just seeing smoke curling from the chimney, voices coming from inside would be enough… and maybe… just maybe they would let me take Papa's book.

Something swelled in my chest at the thought of being able to run my finger along the spidery lines of text again, read the stories that he had made just for me. I would hide it in the small gap beside my drawers that had the loose stone where my knives usually went. It would *just* be big enough.

I crashed out of the final row of trees— and froze. It was gone. The little cottage and the small goat house. Even the woodshed and Papa's butchering shed were gone. The only thing that still remained in the small clearing was the crooked stone chimney, standing forlornly amidst blackened ground.

The odd bit of burnt wood lay here and there, and the huge hearthstone still lay in the ground half buried under dirt and brambles that had begun to take over.

I walked numbly into the space, my feet leaving tracks in the black mud before stopping in front of the chimney. A sob formed in my throat as I made out the small carved initials in the stone at the top of the fireplace, the one Papa had always leaned on, resting his huge hand there as he had waited for my supper to heat for me at night, or watched Mama's tea heat, ready to take to her.

M.P.L

Mama, Papa, and Lyrik. I ran my finger over the small letters, letting myself feel the grief that I had buried so deep these last years.

I turned, walking slowly over to where their bedroom had been, tracing the path I had taken through the door to their bed, then back to the kitchen and finally stopping where my loft would have been, staring at the ground.

Some of that ash on the ground would have been my book. The last bit of Papa that I had clung to, knowing it was still out there in the world, even if it was not in my possession.

I only vaguely heard the hooves behind me as my grief took over, letting the tears fall, hot from my eyes and blur the devastation in front of me.

Hands were on my shoulders, turning me before arms wrapped me in a calming embrace, holding me tight to a warm chest. It was the first time I had been hugged in over two years, and I felt something in my heart give as I sobbed into Darius' shirt.

He murmured to me, crooning in a way I had heard him use to settle his horse as his hand rubbed my back. He let me cling to him, my hands wrapped in the fabric of his tunic and my tears soaking his chest.

"They are gone," I finally managed to get out between shuddering breaths. "There is nothing left of them."

Darius' hand moved to the back of my head, fingers threading through my hair as he stroked it gently.

The feel of it was so soothing, and so unlike anything I had felt in so long that my body relaxed slightly into him, swaying slightly on my feet.

"I'm sorry," he murmured, "I didn't know he had done this, or I wouldn't have brought you anywhere near it."

"What am I doing Darius?" I said, turning my head to look over the empty glade again. "The last thing Mama told me to do was run, and I'm here, years later, because I wanted revenge on them. It's not going to bring them back."

Fingers touched my chin, turning me away from the yawning emptiness of what had been my home.

"You are here because we can stop them from ever causing this pain to anyone else," he said softly.

I suddenly realised how close we were, my arms still around him as we shared breath, but his eyes caught mine and held them, something in them that made my breath come short.

He bent his head and kissed me lightly, first on one tear-streaked cheek, and then the other, pulling back slightly to look into my eyes again.

I was frozen, not sure if I could remember how to breathe as I stared up at him and then he dipped his head again, his lips brushing against mine.

It was a tentative kiss, more like a question, and I felt my lips part on their own accord.

His hand came up to cup my face as he deepened the kiss, his other arm pulling me tighter to him.

My mind was a jumble, dragging me away from the grief of my past and into the present as my body flared with heat, my hand slipping up to his neck, pulling him in. I wanted this. This feeling of warmth and tenderness that I had been so starved for and hadn't even realised.

I swayed forward as he broke the kiss suddenly and stepped back, my hand reaching to touch my lips, tingling and suddenly absent of warmth.

"I'm sorry," he choked out, "I took advantage, forgive me."

I didn't know what to do with the sudden absence he had created and wrapped my arms around my body tightly, shaking my head slightly.

"It's ok," I whispered. "Could you... could you just... hold me again? Please?"

There was a moment's silence and then he was there again, slipping an arm around me and leading me away from the glade.

There was a boulder off to the side… one I had sat on, watching Papa work when I was young and he leaned against it, pulling me against him so I could look over the empty space, wrapped in his arms and process my final goodbye to my parents.

The rest of the trip back to Corvid was uneventful. We rode in the gates at dusk, Darius taking me back up to my rooms before leaving to report to Vladimyre. There had been a few tense moments when Gheata had passed us on the stairs, but she had merely curled her lip in disgust at my dirt and soot-smeared clothing and muttered something under her breath that even I hadn't caught.

Natalia called for hot water after taking one look at me when I got up to the harem and I gratefully sunk into the bath once it was full, letting the scented heat soothe away some of the tensenesses that I had been carrying.

Natalia was eyeing me with a worried expression as I padded back out, wrapped in a robe and brushing the tangles out of my hair.

"You look exhausted," She murmured, taking the brush from me and stepping behind me to do it herself. "What happened out there?"

"Just long days of travel," I replied, noticing the clothes I had stripped off had been taken already. A sliver of cold shot up my spine, half expecting Gheata to return any moment and haul me off to Vladimyre, but as the minutes and then hours ticked by, sitting in silent companionship with Natalia in front of the fire, I began to relax.

CHAPTER TWENTY

"Focus, Lyrik," Darius murmured, his warm breath just touching my cheek as he circled me. "Explain to me the layout again."

It had been six weeks since the trip out to the village, I had not yet had another cycle which was both a relief and a concern to both of us, not knowing when it would come.

"Through the doors and to the left is the desk and library, straight ahead is a door that leads to a washroom, to the right is the bed and a window if I turn hard right... but that's not an option for escape as it is a solid drop to the ground, *but* it should give me light enough to see if the candles are not lit. You will stay in the foyer and let him through where his personal guards will remain as well. You will take care of those."

He nodded in satisfaction, taking a deep breath and holding it for a moment. "Good girl. What next?"

Something glowed in me at the praise, and I mentally shrugged it off. "We will take the servant access down to the lower level and go room by room together to ensure no one gets out and alerts the rest of the building. Once Vladimyre, Kalias, Mihail, and Andrei are out of the equation, your men will aid with the rest, and secure the castle."

We decided on this plan to keep the movement within the castle to a minimum until the four strongest were taken out. The men Darius had silently gathered over the last year were capable of holding the younger of my brothers. The other Drayvn in the castle were a grey area. Drayvn law demanded they would bow to the heir of Vladimyre which— as the last Vasilica standing— would be me. Being female, however, would most likely ensure my safety only long enough to get free of the castle unscathed.

"What if we take this further," I breathed. "What if we take it all back."

Darius paused in front of me, close enough that his breath curled in the space between us, brushing my cheek in a light caress. "I thought you just wanted revenge. We only need to get out afterwards. We will take Catalin and Natalia with us."

I sucked on a tooth studying him, trying not to look at his mouth that I kept finding my eyes dragging to. "And what then? We leave, another takes his place, and the cycle continues. What of the innocent women in this castle? It isn't just Natalia and Catalin. They would just become part of a new harem, and nothing would have changed."

"This was not part of the plan, Lyrik," Darius said quietly, his attention locked on me. "We cannot take out every Drayvn in Mircia."

"No, but we have the chance to leash them," I snapped, feeling my temper rise. "With Vladimyre and his spawn gone, *I* am the heir. Corvin is the seat of power in Mircia, we could bring the sway of power back to the Sylvyns. Make the Drayvn accountable for their actions and you said in your own words that you wanted to liberate Mircia."

Darius face softened slightly as he looked down at me. "I admire your sentiment, Little One."

His finger traced the line of my jaw in a gesture that had me instantly unfocused. "But as strong as you are, you are a female. While your status may be enough to hold them at bay while we get out. Get Catalin and Natalia out, but they will not follow you alone."

I ground my teeth. "How can I make them follow me?"

Darius huffed under his breath. "You are asking a race whose customs are older than time to change entirely. You will have their respect, not their allegiance. The only way to gain that as a female, would be to mate. Your claim as heir would be recognised in your consort and that is who they would follow."

"Backwards fucks," I snarled, earning a low chuckle from Darius.

"You wanted out," he murmured. "Hit them hard and get out. That was the plan. Why the sudden change?"

"It changed when I stood in the burned ruin of my home, without the parents that raised me," I said, acid dripping from my voice. "They died to protect me, a child not of their body. How can I face them in the afterlife without saying I at least tried to change this cycle of horror?"

"You will likely meet them sooner if you try," Darius warned, his hands resting on my shoulders.

"I was never meant to live past my first day," I replied, cold conviction curling in my stomach. "Maybe this is why I did. Maybe the Gods created me, this mongrel of two races, as I am the only one that can do this. I am a child of Vasilica with a Sylvyn heart."

Darius' hand went from my shoulder to cup my face. The movement was so foreign, yet so strangely natural that I felt myself draw strength from it.

"They will not follow you, Lyrik."

"They would follow you though."

Darius› face went blank, then his eyes flared as he registered what I was insinuating.

"You are the true heir of Corvin," I raced on, stumbling over my words as I felt my cheeks heat. "The Sylvyn would recognise your claim, and with my bloodline to ensure it, so would the Drayvn, and we could change everything from the inside."

Darius searched my eyes, shaking his head slowly.

"It would just need to be in name only," I stammered.

"Lyrik," he said, my name drawn out in a low warning as his fingers curled around my neck.

"It would be a ruse, they would not know it—" My thoughts flatlined as his lips met mine in a crushing kiss as his other arm went around my waist, dragging me to him. It wasn't like the kiss in my family's glade. Where that had been tentative and gentle, this was fierce and lit with a fire that burned down to my core, leaving me breathless as he drew back.

"I needed to shut you up for a moment, so I could speak," he murmured against my lips. "It is a good plan, Little One. One that I am ashamed to admit I had not thought of myself."

My heart was thundering so hard in my ears that it near deafened me, and it was all I could do to nod jerkily at him as he dipped his head again to brush a kiss to the corner of my mouth.

"They will see through a ruse though, it would need to be real, and before we move on Vladimyre. After, there will not be time."

I swayed slightly on my feet as he released me and his lips turned up in a wry smile as he steadied me, his hands lingering on my hips.

"How?" I asked when I felt like breath had once again returned to my lungs. "How do we do that."

I was surprised at the look of uncertainty that crossed his face as he appeared to mull the question over. "If it were to be recognised by both sides, it would need to be a mixture of both rituals," he said, his eyes flitting to me as his face tightened slightly. "The Sylyvn way will be slightly harder, it needs to be sanctioned by a priestess, but the Drayvn way is simpler."

"Can you find a priestess that would be willing?" I asked, mentally calculating how fast we would need to find one.

"I could," Darius said softly.

"And the Drayvn way?" I asked, unsure if I wanted to know.

"Just the claiming mark is needed," he said, his voice changing slightly into a tone I didn't recognise as he looked down at me with fire in his eyes. He smiled wickedly at my look of confusion. "Have you not seen them on the women?"

I shook my head, frowning as I searched my memories. "What does it look like?"

His finger traced down my neck and across the barely-there rise of my chest, stopping over my heart. "A bitemark," he said, "Given after the body has been claimed. A Drayvn's... or Sylvyn's for that matter, bite is unique to the bearer. A brand of who owns them. You show that to any Drayvn, and it will be accepted as truth."

I swallowed, my mouth suddenly dry. "Do it," I whispered. "Do it now so it's done, and then we can find a priestess for the rest."

"Not now," he said, stepping back from me, though it appeared to be with effort. "I need to... take a moment to think on this. Talk to a few that I trust and see if this is something we could make work."

I nodded, feeling off-kilter and slightly overwhelmed, slipping into a merge to help my racing heart and mind slow into a more reasonable pace.

If Darius noticed, he said nothing as we continued our training, though my mind was not with it entirely. The next hour passed in relative silence as we breezed through the usual assortment, pushing my muscles to the limit as I was able to distance my mind, letting my body take control.

Darius too, seemed content to stay in his own mind, his face blank as we moved through hand-to-hand grips and releases, neither of us able to pin or incapacitate the other for long.

"What did you mean by the mark is given after the body is claimed?" I asked, panting slightly as I twisted my arm out of his grip and dipping to swipe at the leg he stood off balance on.

He saw the move before it came and stepped out of it, blocking my next blow to his head easily.

I caught the slightly exasperated look on his face before his lips twitched in a grin.

"Surely, you are not that naive, Little One?"

I frowned at him, then ducked out of his next attempt at a hold that would have seen my arm wrenched up behind my back, ducking under his arm, and managing to wrap an arm around his throat with a grunt of victory. I tucked my hip into his back hauling him across it as I kicked out his knees.

He went down hard, but took me with him and we spent a few vicious moments rolling on the ground, struggling to get dominance over the other.

I gained the upper hand after a moment, my legs wrapped around his throat, my ankles locked behind his head as his hands tried to pry me off him. I tightened my core, grinning wickedly at him, at the hold I knew he never managed to get out of.

"Claiming you, means I would bed you," he rasped, "Just to be clear." He pinched my ass as he said it, chuckling even though my thigh was cutting off his oxygen.

"What?" The words registered in me a second later, the shock of it made me slacken my grip for mere seconds, long enough for him to break my hold on him. The next thing I knew, I was thrown off him and flipped to my belly my arms pinned to my back and his weight was crushing me into the ground.

"Still want me to do that, *right now*," he murmured into my ear, and I felt my face flame as he pressed his hips into my ass. "Get it over and done with? As you said."

I threw my head back, feeling the crunch as my head hit his nose.

He swore viciously, which only got more colourful as I elbowed him in the stomach and I twisted under him, wriggling to get free.

Darius recovered quickly, his hand against my neck pinning me and hauling me back under him, then straddled me, wiping his streaming nose on his sleeve.

"That was a good one," he admitted, blinking the tears from his watering eyes.

"That does not need to happen, you can just leave the bite," I hissed, my hands wrapped around the hand at my neck and trying to pry his fingers off.

Darius blinked a few more times, then squinted down at me, raising a brow as his lips curled up in a smile. "My scent needs to be on you," he said, "otherwise, they could refute it."

"Your scent is already on me," I said, mortification running through me at what we discussed. "I'm literally rolling around on the ground with you, I stink of you."

"Only until you bathe," he corrected. "Can you not scent your sire on his women at all times, even when they have not been in his chambers? I have been told it is potent for Drayvn."

My fingers ceased their scrabbling against his hand as I recalled the scent that did indeed linger on the women. Some more than others.

I swore, trying to make sense of the heat that was pooling in my belly at the feel of his body pressed against mine. I bucked my hips under him. "Get off," I snapped, slapping at his arm.

He ignored me, his thumb moving gently against the pulse that had again begun to hammer in my neck. "I promise you, it won't be bad," he said quietly. "You have nothing to fear from me in that regard."

I increased my struggle under him, bringing my knee up into his back, unable to process what his words were doing to me as I felt the blush begin to spread down my neck, and realised I had lost my merge somewhere along the line. I dragged myself back into it, feeling the calm wash of it cool my hot skin as my heart slowed again. Shutting my eyes, I let myself go slightly past the true centre of the merge, tipping the scales slightly more towards a full shift as the mortification ebbed away.

I sighed as I settled into it, opening my eyes to survey Darius with a new calmness.

"Get off me," I said, my Drayvn voice silky smooth in its warning, as I rested a clawed finger against his crotch. "Or you will not be bedding anyone ever again."

Darius grinned and rose off me, extending a hand down.

I took it, rising to my feet and peering up at him. "It can't be now; they would scent it on me too early, and it would risk everything."

"Now you are thinking like a Drayvn," Darius murmured. He was still in my space, but in this form, it no longer sent my thoughts into chaos. "Are you ready for this, Little One? This is not a distant plan anymore. Our players are in position, and the time has come. Once we start this, there is no going back."

"There was no going back the second Andrei killed my family," I murmured. "I am ready, if you are. Find the priestess and let this be the start of war against my sire."

CHAPTER TWENTY-ONE

It was four days later on our usual trip out of the castle that Darius took us in a direction we hadn't gone before.

Vladimyre had done his weekly check-in with us the previous day, seemingly satisfied with my feigned attempts at controlling my shift better.

"Where are we going?" I whispered to Darius once it was safe, watching the lean muscle of his back move with his horse.

"I found one," was his only reply.

He seemed slightly tense, so I didn't push it further, my horse picking its way down the unfamiliar path after him, as I disappeared into my thoughts. It had been a rough morning in the harem. Catalin, who was usually even-tempered had been in a rare mood, no doubt from her growing pregnancy, snapped at Natalia and myself. It had raised Gheata's ire, and she had gone as far as to raise her hand to Catalin , stopped only when I had stepped between them, my fangs bared in warning.

It had coated the harem in tense silence as the rest of the women tried to stay as far away from Gheata and I as they could, and had left a bitter taste in my mouth. I worried for Catalin without me there today as a buffer, and what the next months would bring her. We had come so close to losing Natalia after the loss of her daughter, the thought of having to do it again with Catalin tore at my heart, and I vowed silently that this would be over before she birthed. Not one more child would be sacrificed. Not one more of my sisters.

"I brought you some clothes to change into."

Darius' voice dragged me from my contemplations, and I saw he was holding a pale green bundle of cloth to me. I took it, raising a brow at the dress that I unfurled.

"She is a travelling priestess," he said as if that explained the garment.

I cocked my head in question.

"She has no idea who you are, or who I am," Darius explained. "You are just Lyrik, and I am just Darius, and we are in love, wanting to be bound before our families can separate us."

I didn't know where to look, so I just nodded.

We stopped soon after to give me time to change. The feeling of the dress odd against my skin. I had gotten so used to the rough leather training clothes, loose shirts, and warm tunics that the delicate fabric of the dress felt foreign. As if I were wearing the life of someone else wrapped around my skin.

Even Darius raised his brows in surprise as I stepped out from behind the sheltering bushes I had changed behind, casting an appreciative eye over me.

I was tucking my normal clothes into my saddle bags when I felt his presence at my back and stiffened, turning my head so I could see him out of my peripherals.

He merely tugged the tie off the end of my long braid, his fingers brushing my spine as he did, and loosened my hair from its plait until it hung in waves down my back.

"Don't merge during this, and don't say anything that will give away who you really are," he said, standing close enough to me that I could feel the warmth of his body. His fingers brushed the hair back off my shoulder, then moved to straighten the low collar of my dress, his fingers warm against my exposed skin. "And keep your hair across your back," he said, voice gentle, as his finger traced a line along the back of my neck and down towards my shoulder blade. "Your scars are visible."

I detested those marks. The shame of how weak I had been once, visible to the world.

His hands clasped my hips, and he lifted me easily onto my horse, sitting sidesaddle to accommodate the dress and I let him keep my reins, leading me as if I were a helpless maiden, content to be led by my lover.

By lunch we had arrived at a small village I had never seen before, heading straight for a building on the outskirts where Darius flicked a coin at a man who took our horses from us and pointed to the building.

"She's set to leave soon. You are just in time, if you want the priestess."

Darius nodded his thanks and took my hand, leading me into the darkness of the building.

It only took minutes, the rite that sealed me to Darius in the eyes of Sylvyn law. A simple, small cut on my wrist, a symbol drawn on Darius' forehead with my blood, and the same in return. Murmured words over our combined blood dripped in a goblet of wine, all the while Darius watched me as if waiting for me to back out.

His hands were warm where they curled around mine, his thumb absently brushing mine every now and then, as if settling me, and I barely heard the words the priestess said.

I couldn't even tell you what she looked like, though the heady scent of woodsmoke and dried flowers surrounded her, wafting to me with every movement of her arms.

"Congratulations," she said to us softly, handing Darius a rolled scroll of paper that he tucked into his shirt. "I have marked that with my sigil, should her family contest this," she said, her voice low and soothing. "May the Gods bless your union."

"Thank you," Darius said, his voice near as soft as hers, and then his finger brushed my chin, lifting my face to his before his lips met mine in a gentle kiss.

"It is done," he murmured against my lips, and I felt his tug up in a smile. "You can breathe now."

I felt my shoulders loosen, the tension I had felt through my body dissipating slightly.

"That was it?" I whispered, my eyes following the departing priestess' form as she moved towards the doorway, her movements fluid and graceful, as if she were made of the smoke she smelt of.

Darius nodded, kissing my temple as his hand ran up my spine in a soothing gesture. "That was it."

I still hadn't gotten used to him touching me. The stark difference from the last few years of brutal training where his hands had broken my skin, my bones even, protected me and infuriated me at once— to this. So gentle against me as we stood in a moment of peace.

He must have felt me stiffen under his hands, never quite able to relax and he glanced down at me, his eyes apologetic.

"Relax, Little One."

I huffed under my breath. "You have trained me for years not to."

He chuckled. "Fair point. Hungry? I brought food with us."

I nodded, relieved at the familiarity of the gesture. It felt odd that nothing felt different after what we had just done. This act was one that bound lives together. Mama and Papa had been bound and their lives had merged into one path, yet I still felt the same as I had when I woke up this morning.

I subtly watched Darius after he settled me back on my horse, wondering if it felt any different for him. But there was nothing different in the way he looked at me, or the way he moved that would suggest he did.

We left the village, following a rough wagon trail until he veered off onto a narrow path that wound its way down to a ramshackle abandoned cabin on the side of a river, a water wheel turning forlornly in the water at its back.

Nature had retaken the cabin, the roof was gone, and brambles had wound their way up the walls clutching at it with vicious fingers. But the deck around it was still sturdy, the wood warm from the sun as it looked out over the water.

Darius handed me the saddlebags before leading the horses off to tie to the old hitching post while I did a cursory look through the old building.

It would have once been a well-made house, the floors, now warped from the elements had once been finely crafted, the fireplace still sturdy and straight. Part of the roof still covered what once was the bedroom and the old bed squatted against a far wall, the frame made of thick, dark wood but the mattress had been pillaged by animals, pulling the stuffing from it for nests and burrows. It saddened me to look at this home, that had clearly once been loved, so empty and forgotten.

I joined Darius on the deck, lowering myself next to him onto our cloaks that he had spread out and gazed over the river as he unpacked the food he had brought. The wine was a welcome addition and I accepted it gladly, letting the rich spiced liquid fill my senses before it burned its way down my throat to settle in my stomach.

We ate the bread and soft cheeses he brought in amicable silence, both of us in our own heads and content to stay there, the wine soothing my slightly frayed nerves.

Darius reclined back after a while, leaning against the sun-bleached timber of the wall and crossing his ankles. A glance at him showed he had closed his eyes, his face tipped towards the sun fighting to keep the warmth in the air.

I tensed again as his hand rested against my back as he ran lazy strokes up and down it, the thin fabric of my dress letting me feel the warmth of his skin against mine.

I propped my chin on my knee, wrapping my arms around my leg as I let the unfamiliar sensation settle over me. It was nice, oddly, to be touched in such a casual way. Even Natalia and Catalin didn't touch me. There were no passing hugs or leaning against each other as we sat around the fire at night. Natalia often flinched if I moved too fast around her, and on the odd time I had brushed against her to retrieve something, she had frozen like a deer scenting a wolf. I didn't blame her, knowing what she lived through.

Darius› thumb kneaded slowly into a particularly tense part just under my shoulder and I couldn't stop the hum of pleasure that slipped from me as I rolled my head to rest my cheek against my arm, cracking an eye to watch him. There was a shaft of sunlight hitting his hair, showing up the slight browns in the dark strands.

He still had his eyes closed, but the corner of his mouth had quirked up in the smallest of smiles. He smiled more these days, turning the harsh lines of his face softer and I watched his body relax slightly as he moved to the same spot on the other side, kneading in deep to the tender muscle.

The moan that it dragged from me had his fingers pausing, and a sliver of colour appeared from his cracked eye as he surveyed me. He continued to watch me as his fingers followed the line of my spine down, pressing and kneading as he went, then across, hooking against my hip and then tugging.

I yelped as he dragged me across to him, hands encircling my hips and lifting me until I straddled him. I barely had time for the blush to explode across my face before he sat up, my face in his hands and his mouth claiming mine.

He kissed me deeply, one hand curling around my neck as his other arm snaked around my hips, holding me tight to him.

My core turned molten as if an ember that had been slowly smouldering roared to life, fed by his kisses. My head went foggy as his tongue dipped into my mouth, exploring and flicking slowly before leaving to trace burning kisses down my neck, my body responding to his touch of its own volition.

I felt my heart begin to race, my breath coming unevenly as he slipped the fabric of my dress from my shoulders and slipped into a merge to try to control the chaos that was exploding over me.

"No." Darius› words were muffled against my neck, his lips against the pulse under my ear. "Don't merge, I want you to feel this."

I couldn't have held it if I tried, the threat to spiral into it just as imminent as slipping out of it as his teeth closed gently around my neck, biting down with a small flicker of pain.

I groaned as the merge slipped away and my heart rate kicked violently up as he took my mouth again, sucking on my tongue.

The whimper that slipped from me seemed to spark something in him, his hands bunching the fabric of my dress in his hands and slipping beneath to run up my legs, my thighs, and then cupping my ass. I felt him start as his hands met bare flesh, his fingers digging into my skin.

I huffed a laugh. My underwear had become tangled in my leathers as I had removed them, and exasperated and dressing in a hurry, I had left them off.

"Do you do that often?" He asked huskily, gentle fingers tracing down the back of my thigh and up again.

"Sometimes," I admit, resisting the urge to purr under the touch. It was just so... different... though I could get used to this very quickly. It was feeding a need in me that I hadn't even realised had been screaming for affection. "Especially, if I'm in leathers, they get rucked up uncomfortably."

Darius groaned softly, the sound doing something strange to me as he pushed the fabric of my dress down, exposing my breasts.

I gasped as his lips closed over one of my nipples, the wet heat of it shooting through me as he flipped us suddenly, laying me out beneath him.

"Darius," I gasped as he moved to my other nipple, teeth scraping across its tight bud. There was a pressure growing in me, it made me want to writhe against him, move in a way that both shocked me and felt so... right.

"Can I take this off?" He asked, pulling back, his fingers resting on the laces at the front of my dress.

I stared at him, heart pounding in my ears.

"Over and done with, right?" He teased gently, dipping his head to kiss between my breasts.

I closed my eyes, focusing on the feel of his lips, the fire they left in their wake and closed my hand over his, pulling the laces loose.

He took me twice. The first time a shock, trying desperately to get my head around the feelings that shredded through me. The pinch of pain as he first pushed into my body, quickly overcome by the pleasure that followed soon after.

I had no idea my body was capable of feeling such things, I hadn't known what the rising wave of sensation was as his hand pressed between us, touching me in the most intimate of places, until I was gasping beneath him, incapable of anything except holding on to the earth as it crested over me and I spiralled into my pleasure with a cry.

The second time was slower. I knew what to expect, though nothing could prepare me for when he suddenly moved down my body, his mouth trailing down until he was buried between my thighs. His tongue quickly bringing me to the edge of ecstasy again, his hand pinning my hips until I came. I unashamedly rode his face through the waves until he dragged me up and over him, showing me how to ride *him* until his hoarse cry joined mine.

It was then he bit me, leaving a double crescent of blood on the upper side of my left breast. The claiming mark that would ensure the Drayvn would follow him, should our plan work.

He gathered me to him after we both caught our breath, carrying me into the frigid water of the river and tenderly helping me wash. Taking as much of his scent off me as we could in the hopes to mask the truth of what we had done, until we were ready to play our hand.

"You okay?" He asked as I gingerly pushed my still-damp limbs into my leathers afterwards and wrung my hair out.

I nodded, not quite able to look him in the eye after the intimacy of the moments before.

"Is it always like that?" I asked, struggling with my shirt as it stuck to my damp skin, thoroughly flustered that my body was on display. Which was ridiculous, seeing that he had only just finished licking every portion of it. That thought alone sent my mind reeling as I grappled with the clinging cloth.

Hands brushed my torso and I jumped, shivering as he traced fingers down my sides before grasping my shirt and pulling it down to settle over me. He grinned as my head popped through the neck hole, pushing my hair back from my face and dipping to kiss me, long and deep until I was once again breathless and boneless under his hands.

"No," he said, the trace of a frown passing over his face. "It can be very bad for the woman, or very enjoyable. I hope it was the latter for you."

I really was getting tired of blushing, the persistent heat spread across my face again and I looked down, nodding.

His hand caught my chin, lifting me to face him again.

"Don't go coy on me now. Where is the fiesty little heathen I have been training for the last few years?"

"Can I not let my walls down around someone I trust?" I asked, watching as shock crossed his face. "It gets tiring sometimes, needing to be that person," I added.

He seemed at a loss for words, just swallowing a few times before dipping his chin in acknowledgment of what I had said and folding me into his arms.

I leaned into him, letting him hold me, and for that moment I almost felt like my old self. Content just to be here, with someone that might actually care about me.

CHAPTER TWENTY-TWO

A week later, despite our best efforts at planning, everything fell apart when I woke up to my courses having arrived in the night.

Natalia, seeing my pale face as I emerged from my room had rushed to me, trying to help me slip to the washroom as I murmured the issue to her, but Gheata had intercepted us midway, her face twisted into a smirk that, if cramps had not been tearing at my abdomen, I would have been tempted to claw off her face.

She hadn't said anything to me, just smirked cruelly and disappeared down the hall, no doubt to tell my sire, my muttered curses following her.

I had barely dressed after leaving the washroom when two guards arrived at my doorway. Darius flanked them, his face blank.

"Your sire wishes to see you," he said, nothing in his voice giving away how angry he must be at my oversight. I had counted the days over and over again in the last hour, trying to see how badly I had misjudged and still hadn't come up with this date. He had warned me it could start irregularly, yet I had felt nothing until I woke up this morning to a rending pain in my belly.

"Fuck," I breathed to myself over and over again as I walked between the guards, through the long hallways to my sire›s offices. "Fuck, Fuck, Fuck."

I felt Darius› fingers brush my hand as the guard to my right stepped forward to knock on Vladimyres door and glanced up at him, relief washing over me when I saw not a trace of anger on his features. He risked a second brush as the door began to swing inwards and I breathed deeply. We had this. We had gone over this possibility, this just meant there was no more time left.

My hand reached for the slightly raised double half-moon mark on my breast, brushing my fingers across it through my top in reassurance.

"Daughter," Vladimyre greeted me, that bland smile I detested so much plastered across his face. "Prima Gheata informed me of your news. You will be relieved your trials with Darius at last are over." He closed on me, and I watched my reflection in the depths of his black eyes. "You have done well with your training, I thank you, for playing your part. Maybe with time, you could have improved to greater heights, but it is good to see that future Drayvn females might be worth something after all."

I bared my teeth at him, refusing to let him see how terrified I was. "Any one of those daughters you threw away were worth it."

"Not really," he said blandly. He eyed me over, his cold eyes sweeping across my clothing. "I will inform Gheata that you are to be dressed correctly from now on. I have informed your mate, and he is making provisions to take you. Until then, you are to remain in the harem."

"So that's it," I spat, unable to help the temper that rose in me. "Three years of training wasted, and I'm now to join a harem?"

"It wasn't a waste," he said, nothing in his voice to tell me what he was thinking. "You proved that any future female Drayvn will be worth keeping, and for that I thank you. As well, your mating to Stefan is providing me with ties to the East that I have yet to be able to secure. Up until now, Stefan Becue has been a thorn in my side. I have had nothing he requires, and he has kept his allegiance separate. With him, I officially hold all of Mircia's lords under my reign. You are a vital piece in this daughter, your sons will join my legacy here, and become the future of Mircia. You should be honoured."

His nose flared slightly as he leaned in to sniff me delicately, his eyes flitting to the guard at my back. "Inform Prima Gheata to bathe her well. She stinks of my Secundar, and I doubt it will please Stefan."

I bristled at his words, discussing me as if I were a child, but at the same time some small part of me smirked at the knowledge that they could wash me all they liked, and that scent would not come off me . I dared not look at Darius.

My guards stepped back, gesturing me to leave. They wouldn't touch me now, not now I was deemed part of this inevitable harem. I contemplated refusing, just to create a situation they wouldn't know how to deal with, but the idea of lingering in Vladimyre's presence any longer was worse. Defiance and rage were bubbling in my blood. The knowledge that I was so easily passed on, like cattle for a farmer. I hesitated only a moment, my body half-turned to leave before I swung back, staring at my sire dead in the face. Time felt like it slowed around me as our eyes met and for the first time, I did not feel the fear that had plagued me in this monster's presence. I let him see that I felt absolutely nothing, and saw with satisfaction the moment he realised this, his only tell the subtle flare of his eyes before I smirked and spat at his feet.

I felt movement behind me as the guards jolted, even Darius stepped forward in my peripherals at the slight that would have seen any other person gutted where they stood. But me? I was the card he needed to secure this last obstacle in the east and at this moment, he could not touch me without damaging himself.

He knew it, I knew it, and I let every piece of hatred I felt for the man show as I let my Drayvn blood rise, letting him see the flash of it in my eyes.

"You are filth, Vladimyre. The lowest form of parasitic bottom feeder that I have had the displeasure of knowing, and the fact your blood taints mine is a shame that I will never recover from. But know that your days are numbered," I hissed, my voice cold and low as any Drayvn.

Vladimyre's eyes slid from the spit that was sliding slowly down the polished toe of his boot to my face, a cold smile tugging at his lips as he stepped forward, the back of one knuckle tracing its way down my cheek.

"You think I'm cruel, daughter," he crooned, his face inches from mine. "Then you are going to really enjoy your mate. Why do you think I have pushed your training so hard these years? Yes, I wanted to see what you were capable of, but because I also needed you to survive long enough to provide the offspring I require from you. I have known from the second you were born you were my ticket to Stefan, but if you do not live through your first night in his bed, you are useless." He huffed softly. "I am glad to see you have a spark there, Let's hope that does not die out too soon."

With that, he waved his hand, dismissing me as he strode back to his desk, leaving me in my boiling rage. My eyes met Darius briefly as I turned, seeing the disapproval at my outburst and I angrily looked away, stalking after my guards.

It took me threatening Gheata within an inch of her life to leave me to bathe myself, snarling at her like a half-feral animal as she had tried to enter the bathing chambers as I undressed. If she saw the claiming mark on my chest, it was over. I would be ruined as Vladimyre's bargaining chip, and I would be dead before nightfall.

I didn't even let Natalia and Catalin in, stating I wanted to be left alone, though Catalin seemed almost relieved at that. She had been growing slowly more distant as her belly grew and it tore at my heart, though I understood.

They seemed to take it as grief over my change in circumstances and let me be, though Natalia sat outside the door, calling out that she would be there if I needed anything.

I soaked until the water cooled enough that I began to shiver before climbing out and eyeing the dress that was laid out for me. It was feminine and delicate, and mercifully covered my chest enough that nothing would be shown.

Natalia had a look of sympathy on her face when I emerged, and I felt bad enough for my words to her that I let her comb and plait my hair, sitting in silence in front of the crackling fire.

"Find the best memory you have and hold onto it."

Natalia's words dragged me out of my thoughts.

"What?" I asked, blinking at her.

"When you have to go to him," she said softly, reaching to take the leather strip I had in my hand and wrapping it around the end of my plait. "Find a memory that makes you happy and go to it. Separate yourself from what is happening, leave it in that bed and go somewhere else, then come back after. It's the only way you will not lose your mind entirely."

My heart broke for her, at the realisation of what her life had truly been like and I reached up to grasp her hand, squeezing it, at a loss for words. It only made my resolve harden. I could put an end to this.

Her words stayed with me as I went to bed, noticing all my clothes had been taken and replaced with dresses of varying styles, even my boots had been taken and replaced with the delicate slips the women here wore. A brief look into the nook behind my dresser reassured me that my knives were still there at least, before I crawled into bed and waited.

I must have drifted to sleep quickly as the moon had barely risen through my window when a hand slipped across my mouth, and I opened my eyes to Darius.

"I have clothes for you, put these on," he murmured, pushing a small bundle into my hands.

I slipped naked from the bed, feeling his eyes on me as I dressed on silent feet in the simple pants and dark shirt he had brought.

"Vladimyre is in his study with Andrei and Kalias discussing plans for the east. I do not see him retiring any time soon, but has requested Ellis be brought to him," he murmured, his voice barely audible. He referred to the fine-boned woman that I had barely had a chance to get to know, having only joined the harem a couple of months before. "We don't have long to get you up there; the guards are due to change soon."

I took the cloak he held out for me, letting him draw the deep hood over my head before he crossed to my drawers, pulling the knives from them and securing them around my hips. I merged to calm the rapidly rising heartbeat that had started thundering in my ears.

Darius cupped my face in his hands, raising me to look at him. "Are you ready?"

"Yes," I whispered, sighing as he brushed his lips over mine.

"Good girl," he murmured, pulling me against him in a quick embrace. "Let's go."

We moved like wraiths through the castle, our feet silent as we slipped from shadow to shadow, people passing within inches of us and not realising we were there. Darius led me through the darkness with ease to the wing I had never been to yet knew like the back of my hand from how often the layout had been drilled into me.

Through the foyer of the wing, past the living area that was dark and showed no signs of use, and up a cobbled corridor, the moonlight illuminating our way until it opened up into a larger space, lit with lanterns. The guardpost outside my sires sleeping quarters.

Footsteps sounded distantly down the hall, my sharper hearing picking them up and I glanced up at Darius. "The guards are coming."

CHAPTER TWENTY-THREE

Darius looked down at me, eyes shining softly in the dim light. "You can do this, and I am right here, you remember the plan? As soon as you come back out this door, we move together."

I nodded, running my hands over my knives under my clothes. "I know."

"Lyrik."

I paused, one hand on the door, about to close it and peered up at him. "Freedom," he said gently. "This is what you are fighting for tonight, freedom." His hand brushed my chin, tipping my face up before his lips brushed over mine. "See you on the other side, Little One," he murmured.

I stepped back from him and let the door shut on him, my mouth suddenly dry. This was it. There was no going back past this point. Either I walked out of this night the Heir of Vasilica, or I get carried out dead. Either way, it will be on my terms.

I walked slowly around the room once, it was not at all what I had expected, a large, dark wood bed dominated one end of the room, a desk strewn with papers and a solid wall of books at the other. I ran a finger along the papers on Vladimyre's desk, a tide of information on various countries and even more piles filled with rows of numbers before crossing to the bed and leaning on one of the carved wooden pillars.

I leaned my forehead against it, the coolness of it seeping into my skin and centring me. *I can do this. I have trained for this for years.*

Giving the bed one last final look of disgust, I lifted the edge of the heavy blanket and slipped between the sheets, arranging my body to look as if I was languidly stretched out beneath the cover with a small gap I could peep through.

My heart was beating slow in my chest, my breathing even as I stilled my mind to match it, waiting.

Hours ticked by; the room silent as it waited patiently with me, so quiet that I could hear the wind distantly brushing past the shuttered windows, a wolf howling beyond it in the forest. I ran through my memories to pass the time. Mama's eyes alight with happiness peering down at me with a smile as she helped me up from the grass I had been napping on. Papa, his dark beard shielding half his face as I watched him from his lap, recounting one of my favourite stories. A child's memories.

A voice murmuring outside the heavy doors brought me instantly back to the present. I checked my breathing— still steady and even as if asleep and moved my hip ever so slightly so I could swing my leg out as I needed to.

The door swung open silently, only the slight whoosh against the cobblestones of the floor giving it away and light footsteps prowled in.

I made my body stay loose, made my chest rise and fall, watching through the small gap I had as Vladimyre stalked in, not even bothering to look in my direction.

I lost him out of my line of vision as he wandered to the far end of the room, hearing the rustle of papers as he put something on his desk. There were a few light bumps and chinks as he removed his boots and rings, the creak of a chair as he perched on it to do so.

Then footsteps towards me and he came back into my vision again, dressed in only his long shirt. I fought the revulsion that swept over me, letting a little more of the Drayvn rise within myself to muffle the emotion as he paused at the end of the bed, casually undoing the buttons at his sleeve cuffs.

I needed to wait until he was right next to me, catch him off balance and off guard. I had one chance at a strike and that was it.

He froze suddenly, his head turning towards the post of the bed, the scant light in the room showing the sharp angles of his face as he turned towards the wooden pillar I had leaned on— and sniffed.

The one thing we had overlooked. The one thing I should have thought of; Darius did not know the true extent of how a Drayvn could scent. I did. And this oversight had most likely just cost me my life.

A low snarl ripped from him in the same moment I re-arranged every plan I had so carefully outlined in my head, and plummeted into a full shift, drawing on the true strength that lurked within me that I had kept hidden from everyone.

I struck in a billow of sheets, moving faster than I ever had before, not even bothering to touch my weapons as I launched across the bed to him.

Even with his brief warning, I caught him side on, my claws burying into his skin and my teeth into his neck. I missed the main artery, blood touching my tongue but not spurting as it should.

He twisted, wrenching me off him as his claws ripped across my arm.

White hot pain erupted from the slices, but I ignored them, twisting my body in mid-air to hit the ground like a coiled spring, then launching back for him before he even realised I had attacked again.

He grunted as my knee took him in the stomach, but he didn't buckle, instead wrapping his arm around me, crushing me tight to him, his free hand wrapping around my throat to keep my teeth from his skin again.

"Well, well," he murmured in my ear. "It seems I misjudged you, Lyrik." His hand closed around me a bit tighter. "What a lovely surprise this is, it seems the training you received was not such a waste after all. Why hide this strength from me?"

I closed my hand around his wrist, squeezing until I felt his bones shift under my fingers and his grip loosen slightly.

"I warned you, your days were numbered," I snarled, watching the surprise on his face as I began to peel his fingers from my throat with the strength that I had not even shown Darius I possessed. It had been my secret, these years, feeling it build in me and tempering it down to show only a fraction of what I was truly capable of. "You had no idea what you let into your castle, *father*," I hissed, his bones grinding under my hand. "The second you gave the order to have my family killed, you were dead. Allow me to enlighten you."

I jumped, wrapping my legs around his torso. I let go of his hand, feeling it constrict around my throat again, moments before I slipped my arms up and dug the claws of my thumbs into his eyes.

His hand against my throat convulsed and loosened as blood poured out his ruined eye sockets and down my hands, his snarl of pain cut off abruptly as my forehead connected with his nose.

He buckled under me, and I took his moment of weakness to throw my body weight backwards, my locked legs knocking him off balance as he staggered.

I took a heavy blow to the chest as he swiped blindly and I released him, landing on my feet and launching for him again. My teeth found his neck, and this time I struck true.

His strangled cry was cut short as I sank my fangs in deep, cutting off his air, and then I ripped, the same way Papa'a neck had been torn out.

Warmth sprayed on my face as I struck a second time, even as we fell together, his hands scrabbling fruitlessly at me as his mouth tried to form the words that would call Darius in to help him.

I tore the air from him, tore the blood from him, ripped his life away, and revelled in every second of it. I kept my teeth deep in his throat until his body began to cool. His heart had long stopped beating its sluggish rhythm and his blood had dried on my own skin as I released him, rising to stare blankly down at the corpse of the man that had ruined my life.

It was an effort to pull myself out of the hollowness of the shift, letting some of the horrors of what had happened sink into me. I stumbled to the door, pulling it open in time to see Darius pulling the blade from the chest of a guard and lowering him slowly to the floor.

He spun as he heard the door open, his blade singing through the air to stop against my neck. His eyes flared as he took me in, eyes raking every inch of me.

"You did it," he murmured.

I nodded mutely, not trusting myself to speak as my body screamed at me to shift, clawed at me to return to the serenity of blood lust.

"Are you hurt?" His hand was on my shoulder, turning me so he could look at my neck, stinging slightly as I moved.

"No." my voice sounded off. Distant. I let him pull me against his chest, his arms wrapping around me. "Are you ready for this?" He asked, his voice muffled in my hair.

"Andrei is mine," I replied.

I felt him nod against my hair.

We used the servant's corridor, unused at this time of night, to slip back through the castle.

"Not the women," I said as we paused outside on the landing that led to Kalias and Mahail's wing.

"If they scream, they will alert the entire castle," Darius said, his face like stone.

"Then keep them quiet, but not a single one is harmed," I hissed, taking the chakram he gave me and clipping them at my waist.

He swore under his breath, but nodded, following me as I slipped through the door into the dark landing.

I followed the direction he was pointing, turning the handle ever so slowly and pushing it open enough to let us both slip through.

It was silent in the room as I crept through it, feeling Darius' presence at my back. My eyes easily saw in the dark, but I knew from the fingertip Darius kept on my back he was barely better than blind in the low light.

Steady breathing from the bed had me moving to it, my ears straining for even a pin drop in the room that was not meant to be there.

I recognised the woman in his bed as I crept up alongside it. She was a soft-spoken woman who I had exchanged words with only a handful of times. She lay on her back, Kalias' hand across her throat, possessive even in sleep. He had his face turned away from me, but the woman stared at me, her eyes wide, frozen in place.

I felt Darius stiffen at my back as he saw her and I held an arm out to him, putting my finger to my lips as I watched her.

She didn't move but didn't scream either and I crooked a finger , beckoning her to get up. She did, slowly, taking the hand I offered and slipping ever so gently out from under his slack hand.

I steadied her until she had two feet on the ground before passing her to Darius.

Kalias was dead before he even had a chance to cry out, my chakram slicing neatly across his throat and as the blood of my first brother ran across my hands, I lost the grip on my humanity entirely.

Mihail was next, I wrapped the whip he had lashed me with around his throat, revelling in the panic in his black eyes, his frantic scrabbling at the cords around his neck. Darius had slipped a hand over the mouth of the woman in his bed and hauled her away from our struggling bodies as I waited for his death throes to stop, kneeling on his chest as I looked into his face.

My heart a slow, calm thud in my chest as my attention locked onto my goal. Every single one of them was going down tonight. I didn't want Darius› men to do it. I wanted their blood on my hands, and I wanted Andrei to know I was coming for him as his brothers died around him.

I heard Darius hiss at me under his breath as I scaled the steps to Toma's level three at a time, I was meant to be going for Andrei next, but I didn't care about the plan anymore. This was my war, and I was vengeance for every broken soul that had suffered in this castle. I didn't even bother with stealth as I strode through Toma's doors, my lips turned up in a savage smile as I saw him riding one of his women. My clothing was stuck to my chest with blood, the smell of it sending me into a near frenzy as he leapt off the bed for me, rising to the threat that had prowled into his rooms.

I let his body slam into mine, wrapping my legs around him to stop him from escaping my grip as we smashed into the far wall, the impact cracking the stone behind me and I looked straight into his black eyes, smirking.

"I told you I would fucking kill you," I hissed at him as he snapped for my neck, fangs out. My hand slipped into his hair as I twisted my body, smashing his face into the rock with a sickening crunch. He buckled slightly, shaking his head as I dropped off him, prowling behind him as stealthy as a cat.

He spun and my fist took him under the chin, snapping his jaw together with a dull crack seconds before my knee came up into his groin. I felt the crunch as his balls crushed against his pelvic bone and the explosion of breath from his lungs.

He never got to suck that breath back in as my fangs sunk deep into his neck, ripping the life from him.

I was already moving, running through the castle, leaving Darius to deal with the mess behind me.

Kalib and Emil went next, both dead before they could yell a warning for Sorin who was also on their level. Voices had begun to ring out through the halls now, and Sorin met me coming out of Emil's rooms, his lips drawn back in a snarl.

There was a woman's scream as Sorin and I smashed through the room divider back into Emil's rooms, rolling on the floor, locked in a dance of death.

There was a distant pain as his teeth found my forearm, his nails raking across my side, but it didn't phase me. I landed blow after blow on him, using my body to wrap around his and not let him run from me. I was snarling, a low vicious noise that echoed from Sorin as he fought for his life.

He got his leg between us, kicking me off him and nearly winding me. I rolled as he launched for me and overshot, turning a chair into kindling as he crashed into it.

It was the opening I needed, pouncing onto his back and putting all my weight into the knee that I pushed into his spine, my hands going under his chin and pulling with everything I had.

Fire lanced through my arms as his claws tore at my hands and arms, but I kept pulling, thrusting my knee higher up between his shoulders for leverage until I felt the dull crack of his neck breaking and he went limp under me.

Klause was already dead when I got to his rooms, taken out by Darius' men, and I snarled my fury at them for taking a kill from me. Two of his men flattened against the walls, quailing away as I stalked back past them.

There was one left. The one I had been waiting for. Andrei.

I was completely lost in bloodlust now, feeling nothing except a dull rage as I prowled the corridor towards Andrei's level. A young Dravyn was fool enough to attack me coming up the winding staircase and I made quick work of him, his body left crumpled on the stairs. A second Drayvn I recognised as one of Andrei's men tried as I bridged the landing. I broke both his arms before my claws ripped his throat out.

Andrei›s doors were open as I stalked through them, eyes scanning every shadow and wall for him.

He wasn't in his rooms.

"Andrei!" I screamed his name in my frustration, whirling and running back the way I had come.

The castle was in chaos, men running in all directions as I slipped through them. Someone caught my wrist and I spun on them, snarling.

"It›s me," Darius said, squeezing my wrist until the pain of it registered through my dulled receptors. "What the fuck happened to the plan, Lyrik?"

I narrowed my eyes at him. "You wanted them dead. They are all dead. Where is Andrei?"

He blinked at me for a moment. "All of them?"

"Yes," I hissed, my voice sounding nothing like me. "Where is he?"

"He's not in his rooms?" he had an edge to his voice now, concern lacing through it.

I shook my head.

He swore under his breath, cursing at a man who bumped into him and ran his hand over his face. I saw a ripple of fear running through his features. "The harem," he breathed. "He's gone for the harem."

We both turned, sprinting up to the far wing, Darius on my heels as we flew through corridor after corridor. We burst through the doors to silence, so out of place with the rest of the castle, and in the middle of the room, his hand around Natalia›s neck, was Andrei.

Gheata stood off to the side, a knife pointed at Catalin, her mouth set in a firm line.

"Hello, Sister," Andrei crooned.

Natalia choked as Andrei›s hand squeezed around her throat, her hands clasping at his wrist.

"Get your hands off her," I hissed at him, flashing my fangs at him.

"Now, where have I heard that before?" He murmured, running his nose along the edge of Natalia's chin. "Oh yes, that's right, such a pretty little flower." He inhaled deeply, turning Natalia's head savagely to the side and running his tongue up the column of her neck.

"So tasty too, I bet."

Natalia's knees buckled and she made a sound of fear deep in her throat.

"You don't want her, you want me," I said, forcing myself out of the shift as best I could, reading him for any weakness in his stance, anyway I could get in without injuring Natalia.

I caught the look in Natalia's eye, the dead look of hopelessness as her muscles tensed to move. She didn't care… She didn't care if he killed her, I realised as her foot came up and stomped down as hard as she could into his shin. I had begun moving the second I saw her eyes glass over in defeat, refusing to see history repeat itself with this monster and yet another person I cared for in his grasp.

He barely faltered, barely even grimaced at the kick as slight as she was, but it was enough, just enough for me to get my hand around the fingers at her throat and snap them.

His roar as I yanked her away behind me was echoed across the room from Gheata, followed by a flurry of movement. But

I had no attention for that, everything was focused on Andrei.

The precious moments I wasted pushing Natalia away from us were long enough for him to get a swipe in, his claws raking across my shoulder and down my arm. I ducked the second blow, coming up under his arm and dealing a vicious kidney shot into his back, my knee following it into the same spot.

There was a crash as a table overturned, the distraction letting him land a solid punch to my jaw that made my ears ring, a second hitting me squarely in the eye.

I reeled back, but he was on me, and I barely twisted out of the way of his teeth that snapped down where my neck had been moments before.

I ducked and thrust up, using all the force of my legs to propel my next blow into his gut, then spun, slamming my elbow down on the back of his neck as he doubled, my knee coming up under his jaw with a dull snap as something in my own leg cracked from the force of it.

I barely felt the pain of it, only the slight limp slowing me long enough for him to get his hand around my throat.

I leaned into the grasp, pushing him until he was back against the wall, and slammed my forehead into his face. There was a grunt and a crack as his nose broke, blood splattering my face.

He pushed me off him and I went flying, hitting the floor heavily and sliding along the ground a distance. He was flying for Natalia and Catalin, knowing they were a shield I wouldn't risk. Darius was locked with Geata across the room, the two of them struggling for the knife she held, but I saw the whites of his eyes flash as he saw Andrei charging for the women.

Catalin had Natalia behind her, an arm thrown out to protect her as Andrei came for them.

I launched myself across the floor, my fingers just catching in the hem of his pants as he threw himself forward. He went down heavily, and I was on him, my hand fisting into his hair as

I smashed his face again and again into the stone floor.

I heard a scream from Gheata that was abruptly cut off followed by running feet. Darius pulling Catalin and Natalia away from the carnage that was Andrei and me.

He was still breathing as I pulled his head back, forcing him up enough to murmur in his ear.

"This is for my parents, go to the dark lands where you belong, Drayvn filth." And then I sunk my fangs into the back of his neck, biting until I hit bone. I snarled, closing on it, feeling my teeth grind against it, and ripped, pulling a chunk of his spine out with a gush of blood.

Silence.

There was silence in my head as I gazed down at the last of the monsters that had controlled my life. And I felt nothing. No relief, no elation.

Nothing.

I slowly got to my feet, Andrei›s blood dripping from my chin and surveyed the massacre in front of me dispassionately. I had expected to feel something. Relief, or even just the burden of pain lift from me slightly, but there was nothing. Just emptiness.

Men burst into the room, and I whirled on them, snarling.

"Lyrik."

It was Darius› voice filtering through my conscience and then I felt his hand on my arm, hesitant as if even he was unsure of what I had become in this last hour.

I heard weeping then, looking up to see Natalia, her face white as she cringed away from me, Catalins face also pale as she watched with wide eyes.

"It's over," I said to them, my voice hoarse and foreign in my ears. "No one will touch you again."

I could hear the sounds of utter devastation in the castle. Distant fighting still rang out through the doors.

"We need to move," Darius said flatly. He gestured to a group of men in front of him. "See these doors with the women inside? Do not let anyone in or out until I return, do I make myself clear?"

"Miord." The men bowed to him, and the address didn't escape my notice. Darius had indeed been working behind the scenes.

I looked for Gheata then, saw her lying off to the side with one of Darius› daggers sunk deep into her eye and felt the first twinge of relief that my friends were free of her, too.

More men flanked us as we left the wing, headed for the great hall where the bulk of the commotion came from. We stepped into anarchy. Bodies littered the floor, both Drayvn and Sylvyn, the clash of swords and screams of dying men rang out, echoing through the high ceilings.

I blinked at the carnage, only the grip of Darius› hand around my wrist holding me back from the urge to join it. To rend and tear like my blood sang at me to.

A horn split the air, and I realised with a start it came from Darius, his face a lethal mask of rage.

"Enough," he bellowed, drawing his sword and raising it. "Vladimyre is dead."

There was a pause in the movement as Drayvn and Sylvyn alike turned to us.

"The Vasilicas are dead," Darius continued, his voice pitching across the space. "Mircia is no longer under the rule of Vladimyre, his only living heir stands at my side."

A hulking Drayvn separated himself from the crowd, prowling towards us.

"Then there is no heir of Vasilica, and the throne is empty for the taking."

"Try and take it from me, and see where that gets you," I said, letting the Dravyn see every bit of rage I had for their kind. "Any one of you that wants to challenge me is welcome." I shifted fully, baring my fangs to them.

One Drayvn took the challenge and I had him bleeding on the

floor in the space of a heartbeat, licking the blood from my teeth.

The first Drayvn that come forward was still eyeing me, his face contemplative in a way I hadn't seen from a Drayvn before.

"They won›t follow you, if that is what you expect," he said in a cool voice. "You are already promised to me. Join my harem and I will treat you with the respect you deserve."

Rage flickered through my dulled senses.

"Hello, Stefan," I crooned, eyeing him up and down. This was the male that could so easily have held my demise in his hands, instead asking my permission to join him. I gave him a smile that let him see the wolf beneath and reached to the buttons of my blood-soaked shirt, watching his eyes track the slow progress of my hands as I unbuttoned them one by one.

Sauntering across to him, I noticed people move back from me, some outright cowered as I padded across the bloodstained stones at my feet until I was mere feet from him.

I hooked a finger in the loose fabric of my unbuttoned shirt and bared my breast to him, the claiming mark that stood starkly visible against my pale, blood-stained skin.

"I chose who would be at my side, Stefan. It is not you. Go back to the East and stay there, unless you want to join my sire in his grave."

Stefan's face clouded in anger as he surveyed the claiming mark and for a moment, I thought he would attack.

"Do it," I murmured to him. "Give me the excuse to kill another of you."

He squared himself, conceding to me, recognising he wouldn't stand a chance. His eyes moved over my shoulder to Darius who I felt come up to my back moments before his hand ran across my shoulder, his thumb resting against the back of my neck in a soothing gesture.

"Lord Pendragon." he dipped his chin to Darius. "Congratulations on regaining your house."

The low growl in my throat had him backing away, eyes lowered respectfully as Darius' thumb soothed over my skin.

"You did it, Little One," he murmured to me, his breath stirring the loose hair around my ears. "Your parents would be so proud."

Chapter Twenty-Four

"You hid it from me," Darius said, sitting next to my tub. This was my third change of water, the blood that had coated me was now scrubbed clean from my body as I surveyed the injuries I had obtained. Deep gashes covered my arms and neck, more across my torso and legs though none bad enough that I needed the healers immediately.

I had slipped out of the shift hours before, feeling the dull ache of my body, the sting and burn of the injuries take over the hollowness. The bath had helped to soothe my frayed nerves. Darius› quiet presence had eased it further, aided by the steaming cup of spiced wine he had been feeding me in small sips, the fragrant liquid heating my core and leaving me pleasantly drowsy.

"Are Natalia and Catalin ok?" I asked, avoiding the statement. "The rest of the women?"

"They are fine," Darius stated, his voice tight. "But let›s come back to secrets you have been keeping from me. I would have moved months ago had I known your strength. Lyrik, I have never seen anything like you."

I huffed under my breath. "I thought I needed more control

over the merge, that was what I was waiting for."

Darius shook his head, running a hand through his hair.

"What now?" I asked quietly.

"I have everything covered," he answered, taking the cup from me as I drained the last of it. "My men, as I anticipated, back me. The rest came to my side once they saw your claim was accepted by the Drayvn. Stefan has already left for the East, and I doubt we will see him leave it again, and there is not a single Drayvn fool enough to try take you on now. You need not worry, Vladimyre's legacy is behind us."

I nodded, overwhelming exhaustion beginning to sneak over me. "I just want to rest."

His hand cupped my cheek and I leaned into it. "Then sleep, Little One. Your job is done. I will send servants up to tend you and find a healer for your wounds. Once you wake, it will all be over."

I nodded against his palm. "Can you ensure Catalin and Natalia are cared for?" I murmured, not protesting as he lifted me out of the tepid water and wrapped me in a towel.

He hummed his confirmation as he carried me.

The rocking of his body as he walked lulled me, my head falling against his chest, listening to the slow thump of his heart. I vaguely heard a woman's voice after a while. Catalin, her voice tense but relieved, and Darius low rumble back to her. It soothed me, the people I had come to care for were ok. They were all ok and no one would touch them again, not while I could fight for them.

I just needed to sleep...

I was so... so tired—

I awoke to darkness. My body warm, but unbearably stiff. I tried to move my legs, ease the cramps that clutchedat them and froze at the clink of metal. The weight of the shackles that lay around my neck, my wrists, and my ankles sunk in moments later as sleep melted from me in a cruel suck of consciousness.

My hands flew to my neck, tracing the heavy iron that wrapped my throat. My fingers found the heavy chain attached to it, and I scrambled to my feet, following it in the darkness to where it was embedded into the wall.

"What?" My voice was cracked in the silence, hoarse and raw as if I had been asleep for an age and even as I stood, I could feel the fatigue that dragged at my body. It clutched at me, along with the strange weakness of limbs too long unused.

My mind raced, panic setting in like a cold hand twisting in my gut. What had happened? I had misjudged somehow. One of the Drayvn had taken the castle in my exhaustion and we had lost.

"Darius!" I screamed, my fingers tracing the wall as I stumbled along it. *What had happened to him? To Catalin and Natalia?*

I sucked in a breath, nausea washing over me in a cold wave, making me break out in a sheen of sweat. I merged, blinking into the darkness with my improved vision and making out the dim lines of a small cell, a door off to the far side.

I looked down at myself, the injuries I had taken during the attack healed smoothly, though my body was thinner than it had been, and wrapped in chains.

A pallet bed lay against the wall I was chained to, a bucket in reach and a jug of water close at hand. I lurched to it, grabbing it and chugging it greedily as I registered the dull ache of thirst gripping me. The water cleared my head slightly, washing away the lingering fog and I took a breath, listening for any voices, any signs of life.

"Darius!" I called again, sinking further into merge as the panic that I knew I should be feeling ran cold hands down the walls rapidly building in me.

"Darius!" I screamed, throwing the empty jug against the cell door.

I turned on my chains, hauling on them, trying to break them from the wall, trying to wrench my hands through them. When that didn't work, I turned on my bed, the only thing I could physically destroy and ripped it to shreds, hurling the bits of it across the room.

It was in the middle of this black rage that I heard the lock click in the door and the swish as it opened on silent hinges.

I turned, snarling to face my captor, only to withdraw with a hiss as light from their lantern blinded me, sending me rapidly out of my merge to protect my sensitive eyes.

My vision flickered cleared, my hands dropping from my face, and I met her eyes.

Catalin›s eyes.

She was watching me dispassionately from just past the doorway, one hand resting over a belly that was far more pregnant than when I had last seen her.

"Catalin, what is happening?" I asked, my fury evaporating in a flash. I stood, taking a step towards her and was brought up short by the shackle around my neck. "Are you Ok? Where is Darius?"

"We are fine," Catalin said, in a voice, I had not heard from her before. "So is Natalia."

"I—" I hesitated as my skin crawled. "What is going on?"

"You played your part beautifully," Catalin said stonily, her eyes trailing over me and lingering on the spot where Darius claiming mark lay. "But you have to understand that we could not let any of those abominations of Vladimyre's line roam free. Especially not after you showed us how much you were hiding from us. Your kind is a plague, Lyrik. One that needs to be exterminated. I am sorry it has come to this. I liked your mother, but you have to understand that we must do what is necessary to protect our people. We can hold against the Drayvn that are left. But you? If you switched sides, you would have Mircia in a worse hold than Vladimyre had. You were never meant to survive the attack, Lyrik.

We hoped you would have the strength to kill Vladimyre, Kalias, and Andrei, that was all the distraction we needed to get us out of here and leave enough of a ripple behind that no one would follow us. How the Gods did you kill all of them?"

I felt like I was falling, the ground ripped away from under my feet as I stared at her. My friend.

"Catalin—I."

"You fucked up everything," she choked out, anger twisting her beautiful face. "You were only meant to kill the elders, give us the chance to get out, but you went and seduced him. Made him bind himself to you and take back this wretched castle. Why? Why did you do it? I would have mourned you as a friend, I cared for you until you went and whored yourself to the one person I have ever loved."

"For you," I choked out, feeling like my heart was ripping in two. "For that child in your stomach, *my sister* that would be thrown to the wolves like the rest of your children. For Natalia, and the rest of the women in this castle that have suffered. *For my mother,* Catalin. For my parents, that's why I did it, what choice did I have?"

Catalin›s hand rested against her belly. "This child is not your sister," she said, her eyes flashing coldly. This is the Heir Pendragon, Darius› Son. The man you tried to steal from me. You nearly had him too, until he saw what you truly were."

I reeled back, pain ripping through me, opening old wounds that I had long put behind me. Jagged and bitter as it raced through my veins. I couldn't do this again. Couldn't feel this pain, everything I had, ripped from me in an instant.

"Natalia?" I asked, the name a sob on my lips.

"She's innocent in this, she will be kept safe for the rest of her life for how devoted a friend she has been to me, though know that she is terrified of you. She is aware we are holding you down here for your safety."

"My safety!" I spat, anger beginning to bubble up. I barked a laugh, hearing how maniacal I sounded in the bleak setting I was in.

"I wanted you put down," Catalin said, her tone venomous. *"Darius* forbade it. He is King and the King gets what he wants, but know that I think it is a fool's bargain to keep you alive. However, this," she swept the room with her arm. "Is the middle ground we agreed on. Darius wants you kept alive as with that," she jabbed a finger at my breast. "That ensures any claim contested is void. While you are alive and he is bonded to you, his claim is valid in the eyes of the Drayvn. Until our sons have had sons, and no one will remember you."

I spiralled into a merge, launching myself against my chains, snapping at her neck which was inches from my fangs.

She didn't move, not even when my claws slashed close enough to disturb the air, her hair moving in the slight breeze.

"You think you scare me?" she hissed. "I spent thirty-five years fucking my enemy. I've been in bed with a viper and lived. I do not fear its spawn."

With that she turned on her heel and was gone, leaving me feeling like my heart was breaking into a million pieces and I realised that Darius was not the only one who had broken my heart in this deception. I had loved Catalin, too.

Darius came to my cell next. I have no idea how much time had passed, there was no day or night down here, nothing but the sound of my own heart beating, a sound that I hated so much I had gone as deep into my shift as I could so I could hear less of them, the slow, lazy thump of it still grating at my senses.

I could tell they were his footsteps long before the door of my cell opened, and I looked up into the face of the male I thought I could trust.

"Why?"

I had no other words for him, nothing else mattered anymore.

Darius stepped forward, stopping short of where I knew my chains would reach.

"I did not want this, Little One," he said, his voice an odd mix of anger and grief.

"No, you wanted me dead," I said flatly. "You set me up."

Something akin to shame flitted across his face. "I was never meant to feel anything for you."

I stood stiffly, walking closer to him until I could look him in the face. "And you think I am the monster in this, Darius? I gave you everything." I pulled my ragged shirt across to show him the mark he had left on me. "Everything, you coward. You are no better than him."

His face tightened. "I will be far greater than he ever was. Already the Sylvyns no longer live in fear of the Drayvn. Most have gone east under Stefan, leaving these lands free. No more children getting murd—"

"Not here at least," I spat at him. "You think they have stopped? You just pushed it out of sight, because now you have your castle back you don't care anymore. You fucking traitor."

He said nothing, just glared at me.

"Kill me then," I said flatly. "I'd rather be dead than chained in the dark." I tipped my neck up, baring my throat to him. "You have won, Darius. I'm the last Vasilica heir. Kill me and let me be done with this *abomination* of a life. I won't even fight you."

There was a small sigh, and I snapped my eyes to him. "I did not lie about my feelings for you. Catalin did want me to let you perish in the fight, but I had my men set up to prevent that. And then I saw what you became, and it terrified me. But kill you? I can't do that, Little One."

"Don't call me that," I snapped, baring my teeth to him and shifting as deep as I could to stop the anguish that was clutching at my heart. "My name is Lyrik Vasilica, and I am your *enemy*. The second you betrayed me I was your enemy."

He reached out a hand as if to brush the hair back that had fallen across my face and pulled up short as I snarled at him. "You would have been perfect," he said softly, "if only you were Sylvyn. I nearly loved you, you know. *Could* have loved you. I still admire you, your strength and intelligence. But Drayvn, no matter if they are a mongrel half-breed or not are a disease, Lyrik, and cannot be loved. I know that now."

He stepped back, his face pulling back into the mask I had seen so many times before. Bland, almost bored. "I have you to thank, you know. If you had not come into the harem, I would not have been permitted to live on that level, wouldn't have realised my feelings for Catalin, or have my child. You gave my lands, my wife, and my family to me and for that alone, I cannot kill you. You will stay down here, though I will make sure you are... more comfortable than you are currently." He glanced around the cell. "I am sorry, Catalin holds— resentment for the fact I claimed you." His eyes flitted to my chest. "I will not let her anger toward you affect your captivity."

"Why did you claim me if this was your plan all along," I asked, hating the catch in my voice and the emotion that somehow filtered through even though I was deep within a shift.

"Because I needed it to seem real, your idea really was brilliant... and sometimes it was hard to remember what you really were," he said, his voice softening. "I let the idea of what you could have been mask what you were. I am sorry. It was cruel of me to lead you on as deeply as I did."

He turned to leave.

"How long?" I spat. "How long are you going to keep me here before you let me just die, Darius."

He shook his head. "I don't know," he murmured. "How long does it take the immortal to forget?"

Chapter Twenty-Five

Darius held up his promise to improve my living conditions. I was given a bed, blankets, the food became edible, and I was permitted lamps so the endless dark was broken up. But I began to feel myself slip into a sort of madness as time went by. The only thing tethering me to life was the chain around my neck— my wrists and ankles chains, at least, had been removed.

Guards wouldn't talk to me. Terrified, they just pushed my food across that invisible line on the floor and left, leaving me to my thoughts that were gradually becoming murkier and murkier.

I would leave an apple on a ledge in the room. My only way of telling as the days passed, watching it wither and rot until it was merely a dried husk before I replaced it, watching that too wither as I felt my soul doing in my chest. I didn't care anymore. If I was in here, I couldn't lose anybody else. There was no one to let in, no one to risk more pain for. Darius never came back, and neither did Catalin.

I stayed almost permanently in shift now, the only reprieve from a heart so broken that I could barely draw breath, the pain of it almost physical. A living statue, buried under my sire's castle.

Only the self-preservation instincts of the Drayvn blood I had hidden in kept me from ending it myself. A glimmer of defiance amid the rubble.

There were periods I believe I truly did slip into a sort of madness, with no company except the books that would sometimes appear. I ruined my cell in these moments, trashing it so thoroughly that I would be left in the splinters of it before new items would be brought for me. A mockery of the promise Darius had made me that I would live in comfort.

I longed for the sky at times. To lie on my back and look at the stars, to just float into them, no longer tethered to the depths of the earth, chained like a beast. My hatred grew until it encompassed my soul, and every bit of trust I had ever felt shattered until it tinged even my good memories with a blackness that devoured me.

My soul drew back in that time, leaving the shell of my existence sitting in that cell. Until the day the guard misjudged that invisible line, merely inches across where he should have stopped.

It must have caught me in one of my brief moments of clarity. The rare moments where I wished to see beyond these walls again.

He didn't have time to scream before I snapped his neck. And it must have been the will of the Gods that he had a key to my collar in the loop at his belt.

The last time I had prowled these corridors the air had been humming with the screams of the dying. Panic thick in the air as bodies rushed around me.

Now, there was serene silence, my feet leaving no sound, even with my weakened body as I stalked the halls, searching.

Not one person woke as I slipped in room by room, the castle so familiar, yet so different. Gone were the black and gold of the Vasilican colours, replaced with blue, red, and greens and there was not one scent I recognised.

It wasn't until I turned up a familiar hallway, slipping past guards who rested against windows, unconcerned as if nothing had ever threatened this castle, that I picked up the thread of a scent I knew almost as well as my own.

He had taken Vladimyre›s quarters. The irony almost made me laugh, if I was capable of such an action anymore.

I left the half-asleep guard with a broken neck, propping him against the wall on the stool he had been sitting on, looking to all the world as if he had nodded off before slipping into my sire's bedroom.

Nothing had changed, it even smelled the same, though Darius and Catalin's scent mingled with Vladimyre's faint one.

My heart was a steady beat, slow in my chest as I moved silently around the room, running a finger along the books on the shelf, along the fireplace that crackled quietly. The heat of it touched my face and I hissed silently, drawing away from it, the feeling so foreign it was a discomfort.

A breathy sigh from far across the room drew my attention and I padded to the bed, leaning against the solid wood post at the base to stare down at Darius, Catalin curled peacefully against him.

This is where they had been, cosy and comfortable, while I rotted below them. I moved next to him, leaning close enough that I could feel the heat rise from their bodies, Catalins soft breath curling against my cheek as I breathed their scent in, making sure I would remember it for the rest of my days, and know that trust was a weakness. Love was pain, and no one could ever love an abomination like me.

I had just raised my claws to rip their throats out when small feet on stone had me pausing. I was across the room, disappearing into the shadows as a small child toddled in, fisting his eye sleepily. He stopped, swaying slightly in the middle of the room, blinking in the dim light, before turning his head as if he could sense me there and looking directly at me.

Neither of us made a sound as I looked at the miniature version of Darius, with solemn eyes the image of Catalin's surveying me.

He wore only loose pants as he clutched a stuffed toy, dangling limply from his fingers and there was no fear in his eyes as he returned my gaze.

I raised a finger to my lips and lowered myself until I was eye to eye with him, looking into the flushed, rounded cheeks of a child who had clearly never known true terror in his life. His face was relaxed and oddly trusting as he looked curiously at my eyes, which I knew were as black as my sire's had been.

Something moved in my chest, an echo of a voice that I had nearly forgotten. Lost to me for so long in the darkness. It was as if the moonlight that caressed my skin had brought her out of my dreams. A woman I had once known— and loved.

Could I have once loved?

"Don't lose yourself, Lyrik."

I could feel the ache, deep in my chest as I slipped out of my shift, settling at that midway point as I scrutinized every bit of that child. Innocence, as I had once had, before death and violence had ripped away my life.

The corners of the child's mouth tipped up in a smile and I crooked my finger at him, beckoning him forward. He came, not shrinking from me as he raised a finger, running it under my eye, peering at me with curiosity.

I smiled back at him, dipping my eyes to my wrist where I had dug a nail deep into my skin, blood welling to drip onto the floor, the sound loud in the silent room.

I took a finger, dipping it in my blood, then reached slowly to trace a finger along the child's soft skin, painting him.

He watched my movements with a small frown, then chuckled softly as I leaned in to blow it dry, the double crescent of blood, marked over the child's heart. My message to Darius that I could have taken everything from him on this night, yet I refused to be what my sire was. I would not give in to the monster that lurked inside me, for the woman I had once called Mama. For her alone, I would find whatever scraps of myself were left.

"Go to bed," I murmured to the child, flicking his nose softly when I was done. He nodded and I watched from the shadows as he ran to the bed, tugging on Darius› arm until he stirred, reaching to pull the child up and into the nest between himself and Catalin.

Then I slipped from the room, leaving Darius and this horrific life behind me forever.

I rode hard for days, stealing horses as I went, leaving the previous one behind in return. One destination in mind. A journey that should have taken over five days took three, and it wasn't long before the farm came into view with the barn that had lived in my dreams, both waking and sleeping.

I spent every moment checking over my shoulder for pursuers, but none had found me as of yet.

The sun was setting as I dismounted, tying my horse to the side of the barn, and walking slowly round it to peer inside. It was nearly the same as it had been that day. Piles of hay still lay at the back of it, the smell of animals and silage in the air. My heart turned over seeing a donkey in one of the stalls, now fixed from where I had been thrown through it, but it wasn't Jak, the beast eyeing me with disinterest as he chewed on the hay that had been left in his stall.

I turned my gaze to the house in the distance, smoke curling from the trees as I remembered it.

Birds followed me as I walked the narrow track along the trees to the house, my gaze following them as they flitted from branch to branch, calling to me in their melodies.

A woman worked in a full garden to the side of the house, her sheen of dark hair falling across her face as she worked, chatting to a baby that was cooing in a basket off to the side.

"Ezrah?" My voice was hoarse from disuse and even to me, it sounded harsh in the tranquillity of this place.

The woman jumped, throwing an arm out to shield the babe as she turned, her eyes wide.

It wasn't Ezrah, I realised instantly, though the women could have been sisters, so similar were their features.

"Sorry, do we know you?" The woman said warily.

I held my empty hands up. I was travel-stained, but thanks to a few dips in the river and some stolen clothes I was passable, far from the wretch that had dragged itself up from Corvin's dungeon.

"I mean you no harm, I was wanting to speak to Ezrah, if I could?"

The woman eyed me a moment before turning towards the house. "Mama!" she called. "There is someone here for you."

I startled, casting an eye over the woman again. She looked young, but still older than the woman I met here years ago had been.

I turned to greet the woman that emerged from the house, her face pulled into a warm smile. It was the same woman from before. Though a bit older, her body having settled into the true Sylvyn form now and her ears tipped in points that I swore had not been there before.

"Hello," she said, her voice as smooth as it had been. "Can I help you?"

"Years ago, now," I said, feeling my throat catch. "You sheltered my family. We— they were killed here. I was taken. I wanted to know what happened to my parent's bodies."

Ezrah had gone stark white, her eyes flying over my face, and I saw the moment she found the child in my face that had sat at her table, drinking juice, and waiting for the bread she had baked.

"Magda, get inside," She rasped, holding a hand out for the woman. "Now."

Magda went pale, grabbing the babe in its basket and running for the steps.

Ezrah turned on me. "Leave," she said, pointing back the way I had come. "I want no quarrel with the Drayvn."

"Please," I said, holding up my hands to show I was unarmed. "I'm not here for trouble, I just… I never got to say goodbye, and I'm leaving Mircia. I just want to know where I can find them."

Ezrah's jaw set as she eyed me with no small amount of fear on her face.

"Do you know the terror me and my husband lived in for years after? People were murdered on our farm by Drayvn. When I fell pregnant with Magda, we nearly sold the farm, just in case they came back, looking for whatever it was they wanted that night."

I shook my head. "They won›t come, they wanted me. And now there is no one left that will come for me. You are safe." Her words filtered through my mind slowly and I paused, staring over her shoulder at the woman that had disappeared inside.

"When you fell pregnant with Magda? With the woman that just went inside?"

"My daughter, yes," Ezrah said, her tone shut down and defensive.

I blinked at her. "That was only what, five years ago?" I rapidly ran through the math, the child I had seen in Darius' bedroom had been maybe two, I had killed Vladimyre at nearly seventeen, my parents had been murdered at fourteen. That was five at most.

Ezrah frowned at me, looking confused. "Five years ago? Child, that was twenty-one years ago."

I didn't even feel my legs give way, but suddenly I was sitting on the ground, my breath coming in shallow pants.

"Oh goodness." Ezrah was kneeling in front of me, her hands clasping mine.

I resisted the urge to pull them away from her, hating the feeling of touch on me.

"No, I— it can't be," I rasped.

"My Magda is eighteen. She was born three years after we buried your parents. Where have you been to not know this?" Ezrah asked, her tone softening as she saw the shock on my face.

"In the dark," I whispered hoarsely. I did the mental tally. Eighteen years I had been in that dungeon. I had gone in, the same time as this woman's daughter had been born. A lifetime in the dark. *Alone.* That child I had seen wasn't the child that had swelled Catalin's belly when I had last seen her, that child would be grown already.

"Come. Come in," Ezrah said, urging me to my feet. "Midge, wasn't it?"

A sob escaped my lips at the nickname Papa had called me. I didn't bother correcting her because that had been Midge back then, and for this moment, I could be her again, even if it was *just* a moment.

I spent the evening with the family. I didn't tell them about where I had come from, but Ezrah told me of how they had found my parent's bodies and buried them out in their family plot. She took me to the graves, and I ran my fingers over the unnamed stones, telling them everything I had wished to say over the past years before taking the chisel Ezrah had leant me so I could carve in their names

It hadn't taken me long. There was only one name for each. Mama and Papa. There was no one else that would come to look for the graves, only me. And that was who they were. My Mama and Papa.

I spent the night curled on the grass between them, wrapped in my cloak. It was the first time I wished for darkness, knowing that once the sun rose my time with them would be over, and I would have to leave them for good. It was during that night though, listening to the wind rustle the leaves and the sounds of the forest around me that I felt a tiny piece of my heart mend at being able to be here with them again. I felt like some portion of their souls had remained here, waiting for me. And I had finally come.

When morning came, dragging sun-kissed fingers across the sky I went back to the cabin to let Ezrah know I was leaving and thanked her once again for her care of them. She convinced me with no little motherly fierceness to stay long enough to breakfast with them while she filled a parcel of food for me to take and gave me an extra tunic for the trip before I made my farewells and left for the final short stretch that would take me to the coast— and freedom.

CHAPTER TWENTY-SIX

I traded my horse for passage on a ship headed to Esther. It was the furthest possible place I could find a ship heading to, a land that I had only heard vague things about, where no Drayvn dwelled. Once there, I could figure out passage further away, and keep going until there was no chance I could ever hear of Mircia again.

I hated everything about sea travel, from the cramped, dinginess of the small room I shared with two other women, to the rolling nausea that gripped me for the first week of the voyage.

I spent the first three days in misery, curled against the railings at the prow of the boat, out of the way of the sailors, and heaving overboard. I could have shifted and probably saved myself the torment, but I did not doubt that if the sailors knew what I was, they would try to lose me overboard, and I had no idea how to sail this ship if I killed them defending myself. It was on the fourth day, after one of my mad dashes from my cabin out to hang myself over the side of the ship that a young Sylvyn, barely more than a boy himself, handed me a dried stringy looking root from his pocket, the same as the one he chewed on as he eyed me warily.

"Helps with the water sickness," he mumbled, swiping a grubby sleeve across his face. "Me gran makes it for me, cos no matter how many times I do these runs, I always run rough the first few days too."

It took every bit of self-will I had not to curl my lip up in disgust at the black, wizened bit of Gods only knew what that he placed in my hand, and I seriously contemplated throwing myself overboard for a moment as I sniffed it gingerly.

"Tastes like a duck's ass but it works," the boy shrugged, flashing me a grin.

"Thank you," I gritted as my stomach rolled violently again and cautiously stuck the end in my mouth, biting down on it with a prayer that I would not throw up over the poor boy.

It tasted vile, an odd mix of salt and spice with an undertone of something fishy, and for a moment I considered the chance that I had just had a cruel joke played on me before I realised my stomach was the calmest it had been since my boots had hit the deck of this infernal ship.

I sank down the side of the ship, leaning my head against the railings as I chewed and took the first deep breath I had dared in days.

I threw myself into any task I could in the days that followed, the crew's initial trepidation at a female mucking in with the men giving way to respect as I proved my strength and capability, even in the weakened state I was still in. My muscle had wasted over the years, only my base Drayvn strength remaining, which still set me stronger than most of the men on the ship. I didn't set out to make friends and barely talked to any of them, but the labor eased my mind slightly, letting me work my weakened body to exhaustion each day before I fell into my hammock at night, swaying to the lull of the ship and listening to the breathing of the women around me.

It was on one of these nights where I slept in a fog of exhaustion under a moonless sky that we sailed into one of the worst storms to have hit that year, and the ship went down.

I woke to screaming, snapped out of deep sleep so fast that my body shook with the effort not to shift. I was out of my hammock in one leap, realising as my feet hit the floorboards, the odd camber of the floor beneath me.

I hauled myself out of the cabin, shoving one of the women in front of me and half-hauling another behind me as they slipped and skidded along the tilted floor, nearly falling down the steps as one fell back into me, her fingers grappling for purchase on steps that were slick with water.

I swore under my breath as a rush of it whooshed down the steps a second time, soaking my legs and threatening to wipe her off her feet again.

"Move," I hissed, pushing her the final few steps into the open air and yanking the sodden women behind me up as well.

The wind whipped viciously, and rain lashed my face as the ship lurched again, throwing me into a sailor's firm chest.

"What's happening?" I yelled over the wind as I righted both of us, instantly drenched to the skin.

"Mast snapped," he roared back, pointing over my head.

I turned and squinted through the rain down the darkness of the ship, and made out the outline of the long mast, snapped, half its length lying tangled with the sails and ropes, the rest dragging off the port side.

Men were struggling to cut it loose, swarming all over the remaining masts.

"Cap can't steer into the waves with the drag," he yelled, catching hold of one of the women as she overbalanced. He shoved her into the well under the stairs, yelling at her to hold onto them as he too disappeared into the torrential rain, pulling a knife from his belt.

I ran for the men, squinting up into the skies as lightning forked across it, outlining the man that was valiantly trying to climb across the rigging to where part of the mast had caught, the weight of the felled one threatening to snap its twin.

The ship lurched with a wave and the man screamed, thrown wide into the dark waters.

I swore as I ran to the edge, there was no sign of him in the tempestuous sea below.

More men grabbed the rigging, but their progress was slow and lumbering and I had launched for the nearest mast before I realised what I was doing. I merged, letting my claws descend as I ripped myself up the rigging, climbing faster than any of them could as the ship lurched dangerously below, whipping me to and fro as I neared one of the tangled portions.

I cut the ropes of the first one with a swipe of my claws, waiting only long enough to check no one stood below before slicing the rope that dropped the heavy chunk of broken mast to the floor then leaping onto the top pole of the mast and running along it. I almost lost my footing as the ship lurched, pushed by a wave and rolling heavily.

I dropped down, wrapping my legs around the rigging as I began slashing at the next bit, the wood groaning as every cut released a bit more of the tension.

I had one more to go when the scream below dragged my attention from my task, and I glanced up in time to see the huge wave breaching the side of the ship. We had turned with the swells, the broken mast anchoring us in the water, and we could do nothing as the wave took us.

The ship rose the side of the wave, barrel rolling before crashing down into the black waters beneath, flinging me through the air and off the rigging as it was whipped down.

I barely registered to suck in a breath before I hit the water, the force of it nearly knocking the air straight back out. I was thrashing for my life as the water sucked me down. My lungs screaming for air as I struggled for the surface, only the faintest glitter of light from the lightning above showed me which way to go, and I kicked and kicked, pulling my body through the water until I broke the surface, dragging in a mouthful of water and air before getting dragged under by a wave again.

I fought the cold grasp of the water, my fingers brushing something hard, and I gripped it as it bobbed to the surface, taking me with it. A barrel, its smooth surface slipping under my fingers until I sunk my claws into it, anchoring them deep into the wood.

The noise was deafening, the clash of the storm and waves as the ship groaned and cracked as it too fought the sea claiming it. Screams broke out here and there, and I tried to search the darkness for them, to see if I could reach them... but I couldn't tell which direction they came from.

Coughing near me pulled my attention to someone close enough to call to and I screamed my presence across the water, dragging myself through debris slowly until I felt a warm body thrashing. I gripped them, wrapping my free hand in the fabric of their clothing and hauling them to me, pulling them until they could reach the barrel, but they couldn't get purchase on it, their fingers slipping as they whimpered in panic.

"I have you," I rasped, my lungs burning with seawater. "Hold on to me."

The storm raged on around us as we clung to that barrel, bobbing up and down, going under when a wave hit us then bobbing back to the surface. Every time we were sucked down,

I would wonder if this was it and we wouldn't come back up , but then we would break the surface again, coughing and vomiting water as we waited for the next.

Daylight didn't bring a break in the storm, just that the ship, so full of life just hours before had vanished entirely, only the odd bit of debris in the waves as we floated proved it had ever been there. I could make out the face of the man I held. It was the young man who had shared his water sickness roots with me. He breathed still, but his lips were an unearthly shade of blue and he slipped in and out of consciousness. There was no other life in the water around us, not one voice answered mine as I yelled across the waves.

I had no voice left as the hours crawled by, my fingers numb as tightly as I had them wrapped in his tunic. I didn't even know his name.

Spray from the waves pelted my face and I took mouthful after mouthful, choking on it as my muscles screamed in protest.

By night, exhaustion had taken me completely, the storm had died to a grumbling roar in the distance, but I was spent. I had no voice, I could barely think, except to know that I had to hold on. Had to keep my head above water, and his.

I rested my forehead against the rough wood of the barrel, tugging him a little closer to me, his head lolling on my shoulder. I could feel the faint warm breath against my neck that let me know he still lived and wondered if when I slipped below the waves if it would be painful when the water flooded my lungs.

"I'm coming, Mama," I rasped. "Wait for me."

I sunk into the blackness, welcoming the peace of death.

I was no longer drifting. There was no ebb and bob of the tides under me, though my fingers still ached where they were sunk in the wood. My other hand stiff in the fabric of the sailor's shirt, his body under my hand was as still as the sand I now lay in.

My eyes burned, my skin felt tight from the salt that had dried on my skin and I barely had control of the merge. I couldn't let myself spiral into it.

I coughed, retching, and brought up a stomach of seawater. It kept coming, a flood of water and bile that I choked on, struggling to drag breaths back in. I felt the merge slip from my grasp, and I fell back into darkness.

"Gwydion, call for healers, this one lives."

A woman's voice filtered into my senses to where I had been floating in the dark. I was instantly on edge, merging before I had even fully moved into consciousness.

Hands were touching me, turning me on my side and something was thumping my back as wracking coughs took over me.

I snarled as I caught my breath, cracking an eye into the piercing sunlight. "Get away from me," I rasped.

"Astryd, get back," A sharp female voice snapped, and the hands that had been on me suddenly vanished as if pulled away.

The sharp tip that touched my throat was enough to drag me fully into consciousness and I opened my eyes to a tall woman. She had hair in a strange shade of grey and was dressed in dark leather, her long spear held to my throat as she stood back from me, her golden eyes wary.

I bared my fangs at her, growling softly.

"She is Drayvn." The woman said, her eyes narrowed as she surveyed me.

"Faisyn, take your weapon off her, she is unarmed," a softer voice said. A woman moved next to her. She was exquisitely beautiful, her pale grey eyes fixed on me. She leaned down to me again, her long auburn hair falling over her shoulder as she did.

"Astryd," the woman— Faisyn, warned. "Drayvn do not need weapons."

I lost their next words as my body convulsed in another coughing fit, desperate to rid itself of the seawater that I could still feel in my body.

Gentle hands pushed me upright.

Panic lashed through me at the touch. I was weakened. Vulnerable. I nearly spiralled into a full shift, barely keeping it together long enough to push myself away from whoever was touching me.

The sand vibrated as more people ran towards us. The merest glance up between my gasps for breath showed a huge man coming towards us, a younger one, no doubt his son from the same shade of grey hair as his on his heels.

I forced myself to my knees, the world spinning as they approached.

"Astryd, do not touch her," the giant man said. His voice was stern, but not cold. "Healers are coming."

I looked wildly for the young man that I had hauled with me these last few days— and saw him. He was on his side, his sightless eyes fixed on me, his arm outstretched as if still clinging to me now.

I sobbed. I had failed. I had tried so hard to save him and I hadn›t been able to, yet once again I was still here. Still breathing while somebody else was not. My already tortured lungs seized, my breathing faltered as more water forced its way up and I choked, falling forward as I struggled to get a breath down.

"Astryd, stay back," I heard the man say. "Gryffon, keep your mother away."

"Gwydeon, she can't breathe!" The woman cried, alarm in her voice as the world blackened around me momentarily.

Arms were lifting me, huge hands wrapping around my upper

arms and raising my arms above my head to expand my lungs, golden eyes swimming into focus in front of me.

"You are safe," he said gently, his deep voice soothing. "Just breathe, girl. Healers are coming. No one is going to hurt you."

He held me there, kneeling in the sand with me as I sucked in shallow breaths. I barely noticed the healers that arrived, their hands slipping under my salt-caked clothes, not until the pressure in my lungs began to ease slightly and I was able to slip back into merge again.

I opened my eyes, studying him, trying to gauge how fast he was if he were to attack.

"What is your name?"

The question startled me. I blinked at him mutely.

"My brother asked you a question," Faisyn snapped, and I heard the crunch of sand as she stepped towards us.

I felt the snarl surge up in my chest, the healers stumbling away from me as I snapped my gaze to her. I was little more than feral at the moment, my body slipping into self-preservation over humanity.

"Stand down, Faisyn," the man holding me said. His hands were firm on my arms, but not painful as he turned his attention back to me.

"I am Gwydeon Wynter," he offered. "Were you wrecked? Do we need to send aid anywhere?"

I shook my head slightly, gritting my teeth at the effort that even that small movement took.

"There is nothing to save." My voice was so rough I barely recognised it. I took a couple of long breaths that finally cleared some of the fog in my brain.

"What do we call you?" Gwydeon asked, his voice gentle.

I panted for a moment, thinking. "Lyrik V—" I cut myself off, then raised my head, meeting his eyes defiantly. "Lyrik Damaris. My name is Lyrik Damaris."

He nodded, squeezing my arms in reassurance as he stood, raising me to my feet with him.

"Well, Lyrik. You are in Asteryn, and you are safe."

EPILOGUE

Sweat was running down my spine as I strolled the lines of men, correcting posture and stance to murmured thanks and gestures of respect from the warriors.

It had taken years to see the wariness turn to acceptance and then respect as I had proven my abilities over and over.

I had been pulled out of the trainees as soon as my body had grown strong again and my already honed abilities were apparent. No man or woman had yet been able to best me in Asteryn, even though I strangled my Drayvn blood so thoroughly, that it was merely a whisper in my veins.

I enjoyed the repetition of training the recruits now, lending them every skill that had been drilled into me, making sure that if Drayvn ever came this far, they would know how to fight them, and with the mingled fear and respect that shone in these people's eyes, they left me alone.

I respected Wyatt, the General of Asteryn's armies, greatly. He had been firm, but fair with me since my arrival and I had asked to join their training. He didn't mince words, his 'to the point' communication left me knowing exactly where I stood with him, and I valued it.

Recently, I had grown restless as the years ticked by and respect threatened to turn to friendship. Gryffon, the Heir of Asteryn, only son of Astryd and Gwydion was someone I could very easily let turn into a friend. He was patient and even-natured, seeking me out to spend time with me, asking questions about my past, but not pushing when I shut them down. A few of Faisyn's riders too, seemed to push past initial curiosity about the strange woman that had landed in Asteryn so unexpectedly, gravitating towards me as if they would pull me into their group of friends. It made me anxious, snapping at them every now and then, so they would keep their distance.

I stood at the water station, eyeing one of my latest trainees that had terrible form in exasperation as I chugged cool water, contemplating whether it was even worth correcting him again. My skin prickled as I felt a presence at my back. I turned, hand tightening on the handle of my blade.

"Easy now," The male said, flashing me a wicked grin as he leaned in to scoop his own cup of water. He drank deeply, the epitome of male smugness as he lounged against a pillar, sweat gleaming from the muscles across his bare chest.

I forced my fingers to leave my dagger, eyeing him darkly.

"What do you want, Rogue? Was it?"

A slow smile spread across his lips. "You remembered my name; you just made my day."

"I will forget it just as fast," I snapped, standing my ground. Everything in me was screaming to edge away, that heated smile he had as he ran his eyes over me, an echo of what I had seen before. No fucking way was I falling for that again.

"Then I will just have to remind you of it *until* you remember me." He grinned again, tipping his head to my dagger. "I like the way you work, Damaris, can you show me that hold you had on Kenryn yesterday? The man is still nursing his wounded pride over in the barracks."

"Pride gets you killed, Rogue, remember that."

"Oh, trust me, he has *none* left," he chuckled. "Not a speck. You wiped the floor with his ego."

I couldn't help the small twitch at the corner of my lips, and when I looked up again, Rogue was staring at me.

"Tell me how I can make you do that again," he murmured, taking a step towards me.

I took a step back, my hand flashing to my dagger again. "Do what?"

"Smile," he said, halting his movement cautiously.

I scowled at him, thumping my cup down and turning to leave.

"Rogue, get back in the yard," Wyatt barked, striding up to us.

"I was just getting a drink, Father," Rogue smirked, ducking his head at me.

Wyatt strode up, eyeing his son›s retreating form with vague exasperation before turning to me.

"Lady Faisyn requested your presence up in the roosts, girl."

I felt the familiar ripple of excitement at the thought of going up to the roosts and nodded. "Thank you, did you need me here further today?"

He clapped me on the shoulder, huffing. "No, you have been out here since daybreak, if only all my warriors were as dedicated as you. Go, and don't come back for the rest of the day. When is the last time you had a break?"

I squared my shoulders under his grip, shoving down the surge in my blood at the contact. "I'm fine, I do not need breaks, I prefer to keep busy."

Wyatt chuckled softly. "I never see you spending time with any of the men, or women," he said, his face softening slightly. "There is no harm in letting yourself relax now and then."

"Will that be all, Sir Salvadore," I said, hearing the stiffness in my voice.

"Of course, Miss Damaris," Wyatt said, humour in his eyes. "Enjoy the rest of your day. That is an order."

I took the stairs up to the roosts at a run, enjoying the burn in my legs at the endless twisting stairs and ducked my head into the roosts I knew Faisyn frequented more than others. I finally found her in one of the juvenile roosts, talking to Diyanna and Ingryd, two young riders that I had met a few times.

I liked them both but was careful not to let that feeling turn into friendship, Diyanna had easy humour to her and Ingryd was a calm, stoic young Sylvyn whose eyes took in everything around her.

Diyanna touched her forehead in greeting as they passed me, headed out of the roost and I returned the gesture, pulling my face into the cold, bland look I kept on it most days, nodding to Ingryd as well.

"You know, you could have asked to be brought up here, rather than run those stairs," Faisyn said to me in greeting, her sharp features alight with humour.

"I like the exercise," I replied, breathing in the scent of the Sylkies that inhabited the roost. They were glorious beasts, all fury and muscle, wild and untamed in the best sense. They held no deception in their souls. Fiercely loyal to their riders and honest. I had admired them since the day I had first seen one and it had watched me with golden eyes that I felt like had seen onto my soul.

Faisyn huffed, pushing the questioning beak of a young Sylkie away from the sack she was carrying. "I heard word you were thinking of leaving Asteryn," she said, sliding a golden eye to me.

"I— yes," I said, my throat constricting slightly.

Something nudged my hand, and I glanced down to see the young Sylkie that I had grown fond of pushing against me, her brown feathers bristled, asking for a scratch. I obliged her, sinking my fingers in until I got to warm skin and ran my fingers along it, letting my claws out the tiniest amount to give her the scratch she pined for. I was rewarded with a deep purr, the Sylkie leaning heavily enough into me that I nearly staggered under the weight of her.

Faisyn chuckled under her breath as she watched us. "You know, Sylkies are a better judge of character than any person I have ever met," she said nonchalantly. "Sometimes they will snub even the most outwardly pleasant person imaginable, and I find out later why." She cocked her head at me. "I don't want you to leave, and I want you to stop running from yourself."

I had had enough time with Faisyn that her forwardness didn't surprise me anymore, and I gave her the respect of the same in return."

"This isn›t my home; I have already taken space here long enough."

"Where is your home, Lyrik?"

"I have no home."

She grinned. "Then make this your home. I want you to stay."

I blinked at her, frowning.

"Asteryn is full of strays, girl," she said gently. "We are a mismatched group of oddities that have created a family, and I hate to inform you, but you were part of ours the second you washed up on that beach, feral and prickly as you were. You have shown us skills that have aided our armies, you treat my brother and his mate with respect, my nephew adores you, even with your spiky exterior, people are drawn to you as a natural leader. Not to mention my Sylkies like you… and in truth, that is all I need to know."

I tried to swallow the lump in my throat.

"I need a purpose, Faisyn. I need a reason that I was put here, why I had to go through all I did."

"I called you up here because I have an offer for you," she replied, stepping closer to me. "It is rare that I find someone who I respect as highly as I do you."

That did surprise me, and my eyes snapped to hers as the lump in my throat grew.

"We share the same soul, girl, both of us view the world in a way those dreamers down there do not." She smiled softly. "You know my Sylkies mean everything to me, and I am finding myself needed more and more at the Eerie. The work there is extensive, and I worry that I haven't the time to spread between the two and manage them as they need." She nodded down at the Sylkie at my side. "I chose Freyja as my future mount. She was the pick of the litter and will grow strong enough that the other Sylkies will accept her as dominant, which I need for whoever leads this roost." She smiled again. "Sylkies choose their riders though, and Freyja has chosen you, as do I. Stay, Lyrik. Stay and be my second, help me train the riders and grow the colony so we can protect Asteryn from any threat that comes our way."

Her words sunk into me slowly as something deep in my heart began to meld. A few broken pieces clawing their way back together again.

"Asteryn is your home, Lyrik," Faisyn murmured. "And whether it knows it or not yet, it needs you, just as much as you need it. I know what a broken heart looks like. Give it time and Asteryn will eventually heal it."

I took a breath, Freyja leaning into me, her warmth seeping through my body. She was mine, my Sylkie to soar with across the skies and protect this territory that had opened its arms to a monster and accepted her as one of their own.

I raised my eyes, meeting Faisyn's.

"It would be an honour."

Made in the USA
Middletown, DE
01 October 2023

39891434R00130